Rhody

Addison and Marinda —
I hope you enjoy reading
this little book about
my mother.
— Mary Chase

Mary M. Chase

Mary M. Chase

Copyright © 2011 Mary M. Chase

ISBN 9780979835698

This fictional story was inspired

by this picture of my mother, Rhody and her brother Sidney, which I found in Grandmother's photo album years ago. They moved to Oklahoma Territory with their parents in a covered wagon and on the trail through the Chickiasha Indian Nation Rhody found a golden locket in a tin box of treasures lost by another traveler. The face in that locket etched her heart with love.

Dedications

my Family:

Especially my daughter, Donna, who helps me, inspires m
encourages me in all my endeavors.

Kenneth Armstrong:

A poet-friend and an author, who inspires, guides, and cha
to share my life stories and poetry.

Table of Contents

Introduction

This is Rhody's story.

It begins when my younger brother and I moved with our parents in a covered wagon from Texas to Indian Territory in the year 1900. My father was a farmer, and had purchased a farm previously homesteaded in one of the earlier Oklahoma land-runs opened to white settlers in 1889.

Sidney and I were curious about this new place to live. Papa told us a lot of history about the early years of our country, and how this particular area of land came to be called Indian Territory. He said many problems persisted nationwide between the white settlers and the Indians, so in an effort to solve these problems, the government decided to move some of the Indians away from their home lands to a central location. This was called the Removal Act passed in 1830, and started the land exchanges for many tribes to this place named Indian Territory.

This land was a part of the Louisiana Purchase in 1803 and it still lies uninhabited except for trappers, outlaws, and Indian hunting parties. The government declared this undeveloped land the homeland of the Five Civilized Tribes: the Seminoles from Florida, Cherokees from Georgia, Creeks from Alabama, and Chickasaws and Choctaws from Mississippi. Each tribe was assigned their own land area, and to this day each tribe maintains its capital city.

Some of these removals were nightmarish trips for the Indians. Many died. The Cherokees were the first to call these western movements, "The Trail Where They Cried," later shortened to the "Trail of Tears." This is a sad era in the life of our nation. There were much sorrow and hardships among the Indians, but the dignity of these proud people slowly healed, and managed to live peacefully together here on the plains. After the Indian land assignments were made to these five tribes, there were millions of acres left unassigned. These unassigned lands later became known as Oklahoma Territory, which included a long strip of land left over between the boundaries set for Texas, Colorado and Kansas. This strip of land, known as *No Man's Land* had become a haven for outlaws, because no lawmen were ever assigned to that area.

To solve this outlaw problem, the government eventually attached the *No Man's Land* to the Oklahoma Territory, making it subject to territorial law. This strip of land is what makes the state of Oklahoma look like a pan with a long handle. Today we proudly call this long land strip the *Oklahoma Panhandle*. Who would ever want a pan without a handle?

The name Oklahoma was coined by the Choctaw Chief, Allen Wright, pronounced okla-humma, meaning the "Land of the Red Man." Indian leaders first used the word Oklahoma in a plea to the federal government for an all Indian state, but statehood was denied. Later the government took the name Oklahoma as the official name for the unassigned lands. Starting in 1889, there were several land-runs into Oklahoma Territory, and soon the land filled with homesteaders from everywhere on farms and cattle ranches.

My fictional story is set at the turn of the century, over ten years after settlers had first moved into the area. As time passed, the two territories joined hands in mutual interests and applied for statehood, and after several attempts, Oklahoma finally became the forty-sixth state of the Union on November 16, 1907. At exactly 10:16 A.M. in Washington, D.C., President Theodore Roosevelt signed the statehood proclamation and declared "Oklahoma is a State!"

Saying Goodbye

My brother and I were so excited the day we began the journey from our home in Texas to the land of Indians, called *Indian Territory* in the summer of 1900.

I was then eleven years old, and my brother, Sidney was a nine year old pest, and we looked forward to this long adventure with our parents, Will and Jane Lawson. When ready to go, I still felt concerned about leaving Grandma and Grandpa Lawson in Texas.

I asked Papa, "Since Aunt Molly and Aunt Bell still live so close to Grandma and Grandpa, they will take good care of them, won't they?"

"Sure they will, Rhody, and remember Uncle Mote and Uncle Fred live close too. They'll all look after them."

The goodbyes were long, and it was time to go. We drove slowly away on a three hundred and fifty mile journey in a covered wagon loaded with everything we needed, pulled by a fine team of horses according to Papa. Papa's faithful riding horse, Barney, followed us tied to the wagon.

Grandma and Grandpa stood in their yard among blooming summer flowers waving goodbye. They moved over by the old lilac bush, so they could see us longer as we slowly drove down the road and out of sight. They knew we were going to live in the same place where two of Papa's brothers had lived for several years, but Grandma worried about it not being a real state yet. Uncle John and Uncle Jim moved to this new land several years ago, after the Land Runs started in 1889.

Those first miles were fun riding in a covered wagon following the old, dusty historic cattle trail out of town. Sidney and I chatted about everything we passed, while Mama and Papa quietly talked with each other about their plans for the farm Papa had recently gone to the Territory and bought from the widow of a homesteader.

I brought along an old school book to read, a tablet and pencil to write all about our trip. Oh, yeah, I brought my box of beads and little trinkets. I asked Sidney, "What did you bring to play with on the road?"

"Aw, I brought this little bag of marbles, my rabbit's foot and this good-luck acorn Uncle Fred gave me, but I hope to find some good Texas cowboy stuff on the trail. I sure didn't bring a book!"

"How will you know if that stuff really belongs to a real Texas cowboy?"

"Well, Rhody, if he's in Texas, I'd say he's a Texas Cowboy." Sidney snapped quickly.

"Now, kids, don't start that." Papa said.

We were hardly down the road five miles when Sidney asked, "Papa, about how far have we gone?"

"Well, Son, we're hardly out of the shadow of Grandpa's house. We have a long ways to go yet, but we'll get there. Don't you worry. We'll be there in time for your new school to start too."

"Oh, I'm not worried about that. I just want to get there."

I sighed to myself for I knew this was the way it would be with Sidney. He's so impatient, but I'm really going to enjoy this trip just thinking about our new home, a new school, and all the new kids we'll meet. I daydreamed to myself about the days to come in our new home.

The first few days were exciting, everything was new, and camping out each night was fun. Sidney and I sat or stood on our knees on an old quilt folded close by Mama and Papa's feet where we could see out on both sides. We chatted, planned, and talked about everything we passed as Papa shared, "I want us to make good time each day, at least ten miles a day or more. We should make our trip in a month to six weeks or so, if we're not delayed some way. That'll give us plenty of time to get settled in our new home before school starts."

He went on to say, "We'll have to stop often though and rest the horses in this summer heat. We'll stop at streams or shade trees to cool off, and then maybe stop early in the evening so Mama will have time to cook for us. We'll be hampered by the heat, but we'll keep moving on down the road, though it may be rough riding at times."

He went on, "You see, this road in the beginning was just an old, dusty, cattle trail used many years to move Texas long-horned steers to market. It is more than a trail today, now it's also used by people like us to travel."

Each day was hot and steamy, just as Papa said, but we moved on over the trail mile after mile heading for the Red River crossing.

Stranger on the Trail

As we traveled on day after day, Papa told us we were well on our way to our new home. It was boring at times, just flat land, a few trees, brushy areas and shallow rocky canyons. Each day we stopped about mid-morning at small watering holes for the horses, and to stretch our legs. Mama said it was time for us to get rid of some stored-up energy.

Papa always warned, "Now don't you kids wander off too far. Stay within sight of us. Stay out of the wooded area, for we don't know what or who might be out there beyond. We'll be going real soon."

Sidney said, "Come on, Rhody, I'll race you to that big rock."

"Sidney, remember there's lots of gofer holes to step in. Papa said we could break our legs in them." But away he ran toward the goal. He beat me, of course, but winning pleased him so much. He liked to brag, so I just ignored him most of the time.

A rabbit jumped up, and away Sidney went chasing after it, as if he could catch it. I spotted some red berries along the edge of the clearing near some scrubby trees, but I stopped when I heard something move over there. I almost ran, but decided to just stand still a minute and listen. About that time Sidney ran up behind me, I put out my hand to stop him.

"What'ch looking at, Rhody?

"I thought I heard something. Look, isn't that a boot under that bush?"

"Yeah, it is! Heck, there's two boots. Let's get out of here."

Sidney yanked loose and ran to tell Papa what we'd found. I stood still and watched. The boots didn't move.

Papa came running with his rifle, saying, "I do believe you and Rhody could find a bank robber out here, if one was on the run."

I pointed to the boots, and Papa touch one with the end of his rifle, but it didn't move. Papa said, "He may be dead."

Sidney shuddered and looked away, then said excitedly, "Papa! Look! I see his horse over there. Still got his saddle on, dragging his reins."

Papa said, "Something must have happened to him that he couldn't tie him. Maybe he fell out of his saddle for some reason. Rhody, did you see or hear anything else?"

"No, Papa, I was picking these berries and just heard something move over here, then I saw the boot."

Mama came running to see what we'd found. "Jane, I think we've got a sick or injured man here on our hands. He's alive, but hasn't moved since I got here. I'd better take a closer look around for he may be shot." Papa carefully pulled him out from under the bushes.

Mama put her hand on his forehead. "He's burning with fever." She turned to Papa, "Will, this is just a boy. He can't be over fifteen or sixteen years old!"

"Why, you're right, Jane. He's just a kid. I'll carry him to the wagon. Sidney, you get his horse."

"Can I ride him?"

"No!" Papa answered sharply. "Just walk him over to our wagon. Rhody, you get his bedroll off the horse and bring it to the wagon. We'll put him in it, so he can get warm. He's chilling and out of his head right now with a high fever."

Sidney never left that horse's side until Papa said, "We'll have to make camp here tonight. Son, help me unharness our team, and we'll tie Barney and his horse all together to graze around here while we're here."

Mama cared for the young man while we set up camp for we could not travel on today with him. Mama was sure he had pneumonia. He had no rash, broken bones, or injury that she could see. She treated him the best she could with what she had. During that night he was almost lifeless. She and Papa turned him side to side regularly and put hot poultices on his chest.

Mama said, "That's all we can do now for this boy. I wonder why he's out here all by himself anyway."

The next day, he made a sound. "Mama, he's trying to talk."

Mama leaned over him, "Son, we're taking good care of you. You've been sick, but you're going to be fine." He closed his eyes, as if that's what he needed to hear.

She said to me, "Rhody, he needs food. You sit here with him and I'll bring a bowl of that potato soup from the pot I'm cooking."

While Rhody sat with him, he opened his blue eyes again and looked right at her and asked, "Who are you?"

"I'm Rhody, Who are you?"

"I'm Joel Ray. Where am I?"

"Well we're still in Texas getting close to the Red River. We're on our way to Oklahoma Territory, our new home. Where are you going?"

"That's where I'm going too." He replied.

"We found you over there under those bushes. Mama's taking care of you."

"I must have passed out. I remember being sick, and I'd never been so cold in my life. I've had a cold, but nothing like this before."

Rhody laughed, "I don't see how you could be cold in this hot weather. If you were so cold why didn't you get into your bedroll?"

"I don't even remember getting off my horse," then quickly he asked, "Have you seen my horse anywhere?"

"Yeah, my little brother, Sidney, is taking good care of him, and Mama is bringing you some food. Where are you going all by yourself anyway? Where is your family?"

"Well, I'm running away from home, but don't tell your folks, please!"

"You really left home?"

"Yeah, but you won't tell. Will you?"

"No, I won't." I promised, and then I wished I had not promised.

Mama returned and said, "Well, bless my soul, look who's awake!"

"He's hungry too, Mama." I volunteered.

Papa came back from hunting with some quails and a rabbit, and was pleased to see him awake. He asked, "Jane, how long until he can travel? We need to get back on the road. He can ride with us, if he's going our way."

"I think he can travel by in the morning, if he feels up to it. His fever has broken, so he'll be okay now."

"What's your name, Son?" Papa asked.

"I'm Joel Ray"

"Is Ray your last name?"

"No, I'm Joel Ray Thomas, and Sir, I appreciate all you folks have done for me."

"Well, Joel Ray, I'm Will Lawson. Where do you call home?"

"Texas, Sir, my home is a farm near Sherman, but I'm on my way to look for work out in the Territories. I hear that some of the settlers there are hiring farm and ranch hands."

"Well, we're on our way to that area too. You're welcome to ride along with us, but Joel Ray, since its late summer now, the harvest will be over before you get there. Then what will you do? Your best bet is to go back home, and be ready for school this fall, and then early next spring ride back out there to find work."

I overheard this and thought, "Boy, Papa sure said the right thing, not knowing he was talking to a run-away. I should have told Papa I guess, but I promised I wouldn't."

That night after supper around the camp Joel Ray said, "Rhody, you sure have a nice family. I do too. I even have a little sister about your age and she's pretty like you too."

"I'm going to be twelve in August. Aren't you going to miss your family and your friends at school?"

"Yeah, but I'm just tired of being bossed around all the time at home. I'll be sixteen next spring, and I'm a man now, not a child. Dad tells me what to do and what to think about everything all the time and I'm tired of it!"

"Well, Joel Ray, how are we to learn if our parents don't tell us what to do and not do? Papa and Mama sure tell me and Sidney what to do all the time. They tell us what not to do too. You shouldn't mind that."

"Well, you're probably right, but I hate to be told every day."

"Why don't you surprise your Dad, and just do what you are supposed to do before he has time to tell you? I can't imagine how worried your parents must be right now; just think how worried Mama and Papa would be if Sidney or I were gone and they didn't know where we were. Even though we're younger than you, kids are kids, and when kids are gone, parents worry."

"Yeah, I know you're right, but I sure wanted to try it on my own."

The next morning long before breakfast, Joel Ray was up. He said, "Mr. Lawson, I've decided to take your advice and go back home this morning."

Papa asked, "You think you're feeling okay to ride alone now?"

"Yeah, I feel weak, but I can take it easy and rest when I feel tired."

After breakfast, Papa helped him saddle his horse with his bedroll, and Mama packed food for his ride on the trail. She filled his canteen, and told him to rest often and to drink lots of water.

He said politely to Mama, "I sure thank you folks for caring for me. I was scared." He shook Papa's hand, "Mr. Lawson, I'm gonna take your advice about waiting until next spring."

He looked at me, "Thanks, Rhody. I'm gonna' see you again someday, and Sidney, you've got a mighty pretty sister here. You take good care of her."

We waved goodbye as he rode out of sight back toward his home in Sherman.

As we drove on that day I wondered to myself if I'd ever see Joel Ray Thomas again.

Sick on the Trail

The day Joel Ray left to go back home, we moved on in the opposite direction toward our new home. Every day we slowly moved closer and closer to the Red River crossing, the river separating Texas from the Territories. When the trail was smooth Papa let Sidney and I walk along with the wagon to help pass the time and get ride of energy. It was hot and dry, very little south wind and nothing much moved in the heat, except birds. The blackbirds flew happily through the air from one tree to the other. Sidney and I tried to count them, but they moved about too much. They seemed curious about us.

I sighed to myself and said, "I hope I see Joel Ray Thomas again someday."

Sidney teased, "Well, maybe you will someday. I think you are sweet on him."

"Oh, Sidney, I'm not. Hush! I was just thinking out loud. He said he'd see me again someday."

Papa said, "You two get back in the wagon now, it's too hot out there in the sun to walk very long. I'll tell you a story of how a family once helped me like we helped Joel Ray."

"Oh, boy!" Sidney squealed. We scampered back into the wagon and settled in our special places, and Papa started his story.

"Well, when I left home in Missouri after harvest that fall, I had to cross the Kansas plains on my way to Colorado. I really wanted to see the Colorado mountains. I headed out all alone, just like Joel Ray did."

I interrupted, "Papa, why did you leave home anyway? Were your parent's too bossy like Joe Ray's?"

"Well, yes and no, Rhody, my Papa was a farmer. Maybe he was bossy, but there was lots to do, and we each had our jobs and were expected to do them, but that's not why I left. I had a good life, but I wanted to see more of the country. I had other brothers at home to help with the farm, so I decided it was time for me to go out on my own. Of course, I was older than Joel Ray, and I was ready to see what lie beyond my world there at home. I always wondered what it would be like to live in other towns and places. I wanted to see the mountains, ships on large rivers, and meet lots of different people."

"You went to a lot of places and worked, didn't you, Papa? Did you really do all the things you wanted to do?" I asked.

"Well, yes, I guess I did. I traveled around seeing new places and worked at many different jobs. Then I found my sweetheart in Texas." We all laughed for we'd heard that story many times.

"Yeah, Rhody's got a sweetheart in Texas now too." Sidney volunteered.

"Hush, Sidney, I was just wondering out loud about Joel Ray."

Papa laughed and went on, "Yeah, Rhody will meet a lot of Joel Rays through the years, and one day the right one will come along. The story I want to share now happened toward the beginning of my travels. I wanted to see the Rockies most of all; the mountains I'd heard so much about, so I set out across the Kansas open prairie in the fall of the year. An early, freak blizzard of cold winds and snow cut its way across Kansas. Those winds cut like a knife, and I realized I was getting sick from exposure. As the day went on I got sicker by the hour, and I finally realized I could not go any further. I saw no place to go for help. It looked like snow-covered flat land, and I didn't even know how far to the next town. I was feverish and felt so sick that I could hardly stay in my saddle. I spotted a few scrubby trees and some tall grass to bed down, so I dropped off of Barney with my bedroll, and laid down feeling strange and weaker minute by minute. The last thing I remember thinking was I hope the snow don't cover me completely. I don't want to die out here. I don't know how long I was there."

"Did you just go to sleep?" I asked.

"Rhody, I guess I did, for I dreamed all kinds of nightmarish things and in my dream I was trying to get somewhere else, but couldn't move to find my way. Somewhere in my feverish world, I realized hands were shaking me and I heard voices coming from out there somewhere."

"Hey, Mister, are you dead?"

"I opened my blurry eyes to see two faces staring down at me with big, scary eyes, then *poof,* they disappeared."

"They must have been guardian angels." Sidney concluded.

"Oh yes, Papa, I bet they were your guardian angels." I said.

Papa went on, "I thought to myself, maybe I had not seen anything at all, but then I heard voices again."

"Voices!" Sidney exclaimed.

"Yeah, a woman and an older man appeared with two little boys, just out of nowhere, but I was helpless. I heard them talking as they dragged me in my bedroll through the snow. As sick as I was, I remember thinking of how dirty and torn my bedroll would be. My Mother had lovingly made that good bedroll for me before I left home, and I had always taken good care of it."

Sidney's eyes were big as he asked, "Papa, where did they take you?"

"They told me later that they took me to their dug-out home. I had fallen off Barney very near their door. I knew nothing for two days. They were a family of five, the parents, two young sons, and their grandfather. I don't remember their family name now, but the woman said I probably had pneumonia and would not have lived much longer in the storm, if Ray and Eli had not found me."

"What did they do?" I asked.

"They had nothing but home remedies, but it worked for me," Papa said.

"Once I recovered I learned I was right there almost at their front door when I collapsed, but I couldn't see it for it was a three-roomed dugout dwelling with a flat roof. They were very gentle and caring farm people, who had plans to build their house later next spring."

"Papa, I can't imagine living in a dug out. Mama, can you?"

Papa went on. "Rhody, they told me there were many temporary dwellings like theirs, which meant harsh living on the Kansas plains when they first settled there. I'm sure they later had a good home, for this was a good place in the middle of wheat land."

"When I left, I thanked them all, especially Ray and Eli for finding me, for I may have died right there from exposure under those bushes."

"How long did you stay with them?" Sidney wanted to know.

"Not long, maybe a week or so, for they insisted I wait until my lungs were clear, since I was heading for the cold country in Colorado. When I was able to travel, my bedroll was washed and mended, and I had food packed in my knapsack. Ray and Eli filled my canteen of water, and I think it was Grandpa who put in a couple of peppermint sticks in my coat pocket."

"Oh Papa that was a good story. I'm glad they took good care of you, and I'm glad we found Joel Ray and took good care of him too, or he might have died."

"Yeah, Joel Ray will probably tell his story to his own kids someday, just like I'm doing today."

Sidney said, "Well, from now on we'll watch, for we just might find someone else on the trail."

"Well, Son, we can watch, but I hope we don't find anyone for we don't need any more delays. We need to keep moving on down the road on our way.

Lost and Found

One day a small herd of cattle approached us to pass so we stopped to rest and let them keep moving. Sidney waved excitedly at the cowboys. Papa visited with the top boss man. He said this was a safe road to travel, and there were a few other local roads to use along this way too. He also told us that this cattle trail goes all the way north through and beyond the Red River crossing.

Papa said, "Yeah, past the river we're going northwest on over to the Oklahoma Territory in the settled lands."

The boss man said, "You'll want to follow the west trail after Doan's crossing." They said goodbye to us as they moved on ahead. Sidney waved wildly.

Mama shuddered, "Oh, that river, that's the part I dread! Driving through that water scares me."

"Oh, Mama, don't be afraid. Papa can drive right on through that water," Sidney quickly volunteered.

"Sidney is right, Jane. There's nothing for you to worry about. Besides, we are not close enough yet to start worrying. This fine team of horses can wade through anything. I'll untie Barney and he'll walk right on over to the other side. Remember he and I have crossed a lot of rivers. "

"Yeah, Mama, don't you worry about it!" Sidney advised her, then quickly asked. "Papa, can I ride Barney across?"

"No, Son, you best ride in the wagon to reassure Mama."

"Oh, well, okay." Sidney agreed.

I asked, "Papa, I always thought cattle herds were big. Why are these herds so small in number on this trail?"

"The ranchers today don't have to move large herds any longer since they don't have to go so far to market." Papa went on to explained. "Before the railroads were built, they had to drive their cattle all the way from Texas, through the Territories to

Abilene, Kansas to the nearest railroad connection, so they gathered as many cattle as possible to take at one time. Today the railroads have many established railheads, like the one at the town of Purcell in the Territory, so now ranchers drive their small herds to market by taking them to the nearest railhead and ship by rail."

"I like to watch the cowboys herding the cows." Sidney commented. "I just may be a cowboy some day."

"It's a hard life, Sidney, but that's the only life some know. I've done some cattle driving myself when I was young traveling around and it's hard, dusty work."

"Tell us about it Papa."

"I will someday, Sidney. I think now we need to stop at this next shade coming up and rest the horses. I need to check the wagon wheels too. This summer heat is brutal."

We sometimes stopped in the early afternoon if a good shady area was available to make camp for the night. This place where we stopped today looked as if it was often used for camping. Some days the cattle trail is quiet like the last few days, just a few lone riders, but Papa keeps a close watch on anyone approaching. Yesterday a covered wagon with a family passed us coming into Texas from Kansas. We visited a little while and they went on their way south.

We stopped and Sidney and I hurriedly helped Mama get everything set up to cook supper while Papa rubbed down the horses, fed and watered them at a shallow nearby creek. We rode Barney a little while then let him go rest too. Sidney and I explored well around the area. Mama's supper smelled so good; she fried the rabbit Papa shot, and fried some potatoes. She cooks bread in the Dutch-oven in the fire pit. Sidney and I just prowled around the area until Mama called us for supper.

I explored here and there, when Sidney raced by and suddenly tripped and fell face down. He hit his chin, and right before his face he saw it shining in the grass! He yelled, "Rhody come here quick, I see something in this big clump of grass! I think it's a pocket knife. It is! I see it!"

"Sidney, don't put your hand in there. Watch out for snakes!" When I had almost reached him, I saw his chin bleeding, but he forgot about whining or crying, he just yelled at me, "Look, It's a cowboy pocket knife! It's a pretty one too." He jumped up and ran to Papa talking a mile a minute. "Papa, Look! Looky, what I found!"

Papa was already on his way to see about the commotion. Sidney ran into him holding out the knife for him to see.

"Son, are you okay? Your chin is bleeding!"

"Look, Papa!"

"Well, say, that does look like a fine pocket knife. Let's see about your chin first."

Mama said, "Here, let me look at that chin. Looks like you scraped it pretty good. I'll put some ointment on it."

Sidney's face beamed. I don't think he'd even realized yet that his chin was bleeding. All he could say was, "I found a cowboy's pocket knife."

"Well, take good care of it and you'll have a good knife for years to come." Papa said. "That cowboy probably paid some hard earned trail dollars for it. He must be mighty disappointed about losing that."

I asked, "Papa, if Sidney ever finds the cowboy who lost the knife, does he have to give it back?"

"Rhody, I doubt he ever finds that cowboy, but if it should happen, I think Sidney would do the right thing about it."

"Yeah, heck yeah, I'd give it back. Sure would hate to, but I would."

"Oh, I'll bet you wouldn't."

"Sure, I would!"

"Now hush, you two, Mama's got supper ready to eat, then its bedtime."

"Bed time! Papa, the sun's still shining high." Sidney protested.

"Yeah, but we're rising at first light in the morning to get in some cool driving time. This hot, dry heat is terrible. It's best for us and the team. Barney will like it too." Sidney said, "Boy, I'm keeping this knife right here close to me in my pocket so I won't lose it. "And that he did all the way.

The Red River

Today, we're seeing early signs of the long-awaited Red River in the distance; a faint tree line of the river is beginning to show. Mama began to worry, "Oh, Will, for some reason I'm so fearful of that river."

"Now, Jane! Honey, there is nothing to fear. Just trust me, leave it to me and I'll get us through this. You and the kids will be safe. This is the well known Noah's crossing where hundreds of cattle have crossed for years. It's a well-worn path."

We drove on and later in the morning we saw the wide river. Mama said, "Oh, my goodness, Will. Look!"

"Yes, it is wide in places, but it's not too deep right here where we cross. Moving water is just scary, but trust me, Jane."

The crossing came into actual view, Mama really panicked. Even Sidney's big eyes shined with fear, and he stayed quiet for a change. Papa told us again that the water was not too deep or swift at this crossing where the cattle trail slips into the river.

Mama said quietly to herself, "I've dreaded this day the whole trip, and today we are here!" Papa reassured her again, that it will be over soon.

Mama said, "Oh my, Will, I'm so scared! I've never been so scared."

"Jane, don't worry, put your feet here to brace yourself and just hold on tight for the crossing itself will happen quick. The kids are safe here in the bed of the wagon right beside you. We are here at the right time of day, and the water is quiet. I've tied down everything hanging on the wagon, so we won't lose anything."

The team slowly eased the wagon up close to the edge and Papa got out of the wagon; he stood watching the water a few minutes and all the surroundings before starting the crossing.

"Mama, don't be afraid. Papa trusts our horses. He says they are not skittish at all." I repeated to her again what Papa had just said.

Papa came over to Mama and said, "Now Jane I want you to watch Barney." I'll untie him and he will walk straight across the river and wait for us on the other side. We will see where he crosses in the water, and our team will follow him." We quietly watched Papa lead Barney to the edge of the water, where he patted his rear, Barney snorted once or twice and obediently waded into the water.

Papa climbed into the wagon seated beside Mama to watch. He said, "Jane, now watch, there Barney goes across. Barney and I have crossed rivers like this before, and he knows what to do."

We all sat spellbound watching Barney do exactly as Papa said he would do. He rapidly crossed over, stumbling several times on the rocks and holes underfoot, then moved on through the water and upon the dry shoreline dripping with that red, muddy water. He stopped and waited. He looked back to see Papa. He stood still.

Papa didn't hesitate. He said, "Gitty-up" to the team and they eased off down to the water's edge. They snorted and stepped quickly into the water.

43

Papa urged them on and aimed for Barney's path. They obeyed his commands and followed the path straight across the moving water. The wagon bounced over rocks, high and low places, as it jerked back and forth splashing water. The horses stumbled as they stepped in holes and over rocks, but never slowed their pace. They just pulled harder as the wagon tilted and leaned in the uneven places. Sidney and I sat on our knees clinging to the sideboards of the wagon close to Mama's feet, listening to the rattle of everything about us. Mama gasped at every jerky movement, but Papa kept urging the horses onward. We crossed slowly bumping over every chug hole and rock at an even gait; the horses snorted and pulled and never hesitated until we were all the way across. Our eyes were big and somber as we sat watching every splash against the wagon. Even Sidney sat speechless.

The wagon wheels in the red mud picked up their tracks when we came up out of the water onto the sticky, muddy shore. The horses pulled hard with their strong shoulders against the harness dragging the wet, dripping wagon free from the water; they never eased up one time until we were completely out onto the dry shore. Papa said, "Whoa," and we stopped very near where Barney stood waiting.

Papa looked at Mama, "See Jane, I told you it would all go smoothly." She smiled with a big sigh of relief.

"Oh, Will, I was so scared!"

Sidney said, "Yeah, Mama, it was just like Papa said."

"Oh, Will, I'm so glad to be on the other side of that river."

Papa quickly asked me and Sidney, "Hey, kids, where are we now?"

Sidney guessed, "The other side of the river?"

Papa laughed, "Well, we are on the other side of the river, but we are now in Indian land. We're in the land of the Chickasaw Indian Nation! This is one of the Five Civilized Tribes who relocated here in the mid-eighteen hundreds from Mississippi. They've lived in this area a long time. This is their land!"

Sidney and I shuddered just knowing we were at last in Indian Territory. "Do they care if we cross their land?" I asked.

"No they don't mind at all for us to drive through their land."

We stopped to rest the team. They had snorted and breathed hard for the last few minutes on this dry cattle trail beyond the river. Papa checked over the wagon wheels too before we traveled on northward.

He said, "We'll drive on until we find a good shady place to set up camp for tonight. Then tomorrow we'll leave this cattle trail and start a more northwestern direction over the rough, unknown turf of Indian land."

"Why Papa, this is a good road?" Sidney asked.

"Son, the cattle trail we've been on splits after the crossing, one goes off to the east from here and we want to go west from here, so we will part ways from this cattle trail."

Sidney and I crouched quietly, peering over the edge of the wagon like two raccoons. Our thoughts had flipped from cowboys and robbers on the cattle trail to Indians. Papa drove onward and searched for a good shady place to set up camp for the night. Sidney and I saw everything that moved as we slowly rolled along in the Chickasaw Indian Nation.

Campsite in Indian Land

Papa softly whistled a tune over and over to himself after we entered Indian Territory. Our thoughts of Indians had subdued us. We drove on north on the cattle trail a short ways, and then angled off westward just as Papa had said. We drove some distance before reaching a good overnight campsite. Finally we spotted a shady grove of trees not far from a little Indian town called Wapanucka. Papa drove under the edge of this canopy of shade and stopped. An eerie silence hovered in its coolness. All we heard were birds fluttering away at our presence, and strange unknown sounds coming from a distance over the nearby hills.

Papa scanned the area around us to be sure we were alone, and then Sidney and I jumped out of the wagon. Mama needed wood for a campfire to make our supper, so we scurried about gathering wood. Our steps crunched like giants walking through dried leaves and twigs all around, while Papa took care of Barney and the team. He staked them out, so they could graze on the nice green clumps of prairie grass.

After we finished helping Mama, Sidney and I nosed around nearby in the cool shade, for we were curious about this strange Indian land. Sidney spotted a squirrel scamper up a tree, so he ran toward the tree, when all of a sudden he wheeled around and ran toward me screeching loudly, "Rhode-e-e! What does he want?"

I glanced up to see an old Indian man and a golden colored dog walking slowly toward us from the edge of the shade. I ran over to Sidney and muzzled his mouth with my hand. "How should I know? Be quiet! Maybe this is his land or something." We both raced back to the wagon where Papa was unloading some things. Sidney stumbled, but I yanked him back upon his feet and away we went to camp.

We watched the Indian and his dog walk slowly into our shady grove. They both appeared exhausted from the heat. He waved a shaky hand to Papa and stopped at a nearby tree and sat down. He leaned back against the tree to rest with his dog's head resting on his leg. Papa took water to them and they both drank some water, but just nodded as if they were not interested in the food Papa offered to them. He held up a little bag of something and nodded his thanks to Papa.

Sidney was terrified of them. I was scared too, especially when he curiously shifted his eyes toward us.

"Papa," I bravely said, "I'm kind of afraid of him, but Sidney is shaking. Papa, does he remind you a little of Grandpa."

"Well, yeah, I guess he does walk a little like Grandpa. Rhody, he is just a tired, old man right now."

Sidney said, "But I wish he would go on home to his house."

We watched them while we quietly ate our supper, and before darkness enfolded the area, Papa examined the whole area again for signs of anyone else lurking around. The old Indian settled down to sleep, and his dog sat watching us.

Sidney finally whispered, "Papa, do you think they are following us?"

"No, Son I'm sure they live around here somewhere close, and just got tired, so they stopped to rest. They'll go on home after awhile."

Mama was apprehensive too about the Indian's presence, so Papa said he'd watch.

He said, "Go on to bed, all of you, and I'll keep watch on them for a while."

The next morning when the early sun hit my face, I woke up and my eyes flashed first to the tree. I squealed, "Papa! Papa, they're gone!"

I startled Papa awake. He confessed, "I guess I dozed off, for they were still here just before dawn."

Sidney woke up too and we both ran to the tree where they had slept. The only thing there was their bag of berries and nuts. I grabbed it and ran to show Mama, "Look, the Indian left us a bag of berries and nuts."

She insisted we put it back right then, saying, "They'll be back for it." As we ate breakfast, questions flew with every bite, even Mama confessed that she was puzzled about the visit of the Indian and his dog. Sidney and I were certainly full of questions about our guests.

Sidney asked, "I just want to know why they came and stayed with us?" Why didn't they go on home to sleep?"

"Yeah, and why did they leave so early this morning anyway? Why did they just leave without talking to us?"

Mama replied by trying to reassure us, "Well, all we know now is that they are both gone. I don't think we will ever see them again or know why they stayed so close with us, so let's not worry about it anymore. Let's just eat our breakfast."

Papa said "Well, I think he was just a tired, old Indian man with his dog who needed to stop and rest for the night. They have probably gone on home now wherever that is. Remember this is their homeland, so let's finish eating, load up and hit the trail. We still have a long journey yet ahead of us."

We helped load up everything quickly after we ate, and were ready to start on our way. I glanced back at the grove one last time as our wagon rolled away. I shouted, "Papa, wait! The golden dog is back. The old Indian left his dog."

Papa stopped to look and I asked, "Papa, can he come with us" Please, please, Papa, may I call him?"

"Please, Papa!" Sidney chimed in.

"No! No to both of you! He belongs to the old Indian man, and he'll be back for him. He is a fine looking dog and they've probably been companions for a long time."

The dog stood wagging his tail as we drove out of sight. I sighed, "Oh, I wish he was our dog."

"Me, too!" Sidney said.

As we drove away I kept watching and was so disappointed that the golden dog did not come along with us. We puzzled over and over about this incident and then I said, "Mama, I think I know who that Indian is."

Big-ears-Sidney butted in, "Who, Rhody, who is he?"

"I think he was our Guardian Angel!"

"Our what?" Sidney snarled. "Aw, Rhody, you know Guardian Angels are not Indians and they don't have dogs."

"Well, I believe they were our Guardian Angels last night. You know Mama always tells us that our Guardian Angels look after us."

"Well, Rhody, you just might be right." Mama agreed. "We don't always know when we need their protection, so maybe we needed them last night. Remember, we pray for God's protection every night, don't we?"

"Protection from what?" Sidney asked.

"Well, we don't know! We may never know." I answered.

Mama and Papa listened to our reasoning, then Papa laughed and spoke up, "Well, if that's who they are, I hope they help lead us through the rest of this Indian land, for I could sure use some help right about now."

We rolled on over this quiet, strange land heading west with Papa saying over and over that he remembers a well-traveled road through here somewhere when he went to the Territories to buy our house and land, and this doesn't seem to be it.

Traveling On

After we left the Indian campsite, we traveled toward the west through this uncharted land. This road was over the rough unknown turf of the Indians. Sidney and I settled down in the wagon crouching quietly by Mama's feet looking over the sides like two raccoons. Rocks and grassy clumps spread before us and low hills surrounded us, as the wagon jostled and jerked along. The leather harness on the horses squeaked in rhythm, while their sweaty smells reeked in the summer air.

Papa's brown eyes watched intently and his face showed concern, because he knew this was not what he had remembered. There were no established roads or prairie landmarks for him to follow. Mama watched closely too for gullies and deep ditches to avoid. A curious silence fell over us. Papa was quiet and edgy, while we all stared around and listened; Papa's inner compass worked overtime. The wagon creaked with abuse. Heavy breathing and loud snorts came from the horses, as if they also sensed our uneasiness.

I really thought I saw something move, but didn't say anything. I asked Papa, "Will we really see Indians here?"

"Sure, Rhody, this is Indian Territory that we are traveling through right now to reach our new home. Yes, we will see Indians, but there's nothing to fear from them."

"But, Papa, I thought I saw something move back there."

Sidney popped up, "Papa, did you see anything?"

"No, Son, I think Rhody's imagination is working overtime today. There is nothing to fear on this road. These Indians are all friendly."

"Well, then if Papa is not afraid, neither am I." I stated.

Sidney whispered, "But, Rhody, did you really see something back there?"

"Yes, I saw a shadow move."

Papa said, "You could have seen a coyote or wild dog."

"But Papa, could an Indian be following us?"

"It's not likely, unless out of curiosity," he replied.

I said, "Well, I'm sure I saw a shadow."

"Now, Rhody, let's say no more about this. There's no one following us, so don't scare your brother."

I knew Papa was serious so we settled down to watch the horizon of rolling hills encircling us, dotted by squatty trees and grasses growing in the red soil. Papa's concern mounted at the sight of perfect hiding places among the rocky ridges and red canyons appearing in the distance.

"There!" I gasp, pointing to a shadow in a sand plum thicket by some rocks. I tried to keep quiet, but couldn't. I yanked on Mama's skirt and motioned.

She quickly glanced. "Rhody, I don't see a thing.

Papa finally said, "We'll rest the horses at the top of that next hill, and look around from there. Maybe we can find Rhody's phantom out there somewhere."

"What's a phantom, Papa?"

"It's something you see, that's not there." He teased.

Once out of the wagon, Sidney and I scattered like bats and frolicked like two wild mustangs on the prairie. We forgot all about being in the land of Indians. Sidney was my shadow as lizards dodged our feet, birds and jackrabbits jumped and disappeared like magic at our commotion. We explored all around the wagon then I raced on ahead of Sidney. Suddenly, something rustled in the tall bushes before me. I saw eyes through the grass.

I stopped with heavy feet like rocks. My mouth flew open, but made no sound until Sidney bumped into me. I grabbed his hand and we ran for the wagon yelling, Papa! Papa!" He came running with his rifle.

I shouted, "It's no phantom, Papa! I really saw eyes watching us from over there."

"Hurry! You kids get back in the wagon, and let's get out of here! I'm sure it's wild dogs, and they can be vicious if they are hungry."

Racing to the wagon, Sidney scampered aboard first like a squirrel. The horses moved quickly at Papa's command, saying, "I'm sure it's dogs."

"But Papa, I didn't see any dogs. I just saw two eyes."

We rode on quietly. I didn't want to say anything else for Papa was upset. Time passed in uneventful hours. I saw no more evidence of our phantom follower. I guess he kept low, and that's good, for I knew Papa would not tolerate any more of my *nonsense* about being followed.

On and on we traveled . . . then again I saw something move among some tall grasses. I didn't say anything then. I just kept watching. Something, like a shadow moved behind a tree. I motioned toward the tree.

Papa glanced over there but kept driving, as he watched closely in that direction as we passed.

"Rhody, I don't see a thing."

"Just watch, Papa, I saw something by that tree back there."

Holding tightly onto the side boards of the wagon, Sidney and I again huddled by Mama's feet on our old folded quilt. Sidney pushed back his straw hat and whispered, "Rhody, did you really see something back there by that big tree or are you just jokin' us?"

"Yes, I did see something. I saw a shadow move!"

Sidney quickly asked, "Papa, did you see anything?"

"No, Son, Rhody's imagination is working overtime again."

Sidney shuddered. "Papa, is she seeing those *phantoms* again or is someone really following us?"

"No, Son, no one is following us. Now Rhody, let's hush this nonsense. You've seen too many shadows already. There is truly nothing that should cause you to worry like this. Just remember we are getting closer every day to our new home and all those new friends. You both will enjoy our new home. You and Sidney will each have a bedroom all to yourself."

Sidney asked, "Is my bedroom close to yours and Mama's?"

"Right next door." Papa said.

Sidney was relieved. "Look Rhody," pointing to some ripe plums. "I'm getting hungry for a plum pudding, aren't you?"

Mama said, "We'll stop and pick some before we camp for the night." So we rolled on looking for the next plum thicket.

The Prairie Guardian

Sidney and I often remembered the presence of the Indian and his dog with us that first night in Indian land and wondered where they might be now.

"I still wish his dog had come with us." I said occasionally.

"Me too," Sidney echoed.

Papa said, "Hey, kids, keep your thoughts on our new home, so let's forget the dog and shadows out there and enjoy what's here now. We'll get a dog once we get there and get settled"

"O boy!" Sidney loudly agreed.

"Yeah, come on Sidney, let's just help Papa watch for rocks and clumps in the road," but in my heart I still wished the golden dog had come with us.

As we drove I still secretly watched behind every bush and over every hill hoping to see him behind us somewhere. When we drove away the dog stood waging his tail like he really wanted to come with us. That was a scene I could not get out of my mind, so at times I still felt sad and disappointed that he did not come. Papa explained that the dog and the old Indian were good friends, and had probably been together for a long time, but I kept remembering his waging tail.

Papa's horse, Barney, who was tied to the back of the wagon or sometimes to the side, listened as we talked to him and I watched his ears move around back and forth to listen better. When his ears heard unfamiliar sounds they perked up like he was listening and waiting for something unusual to happen. When a rabbit jumped up anywhere near or any unusual movements in the tall grass his ears turned to that direction. I always looked too. There were small groves of trees, tall grass and weeds, rocky mounds and all kinds of underbrush on this rough ground we used as a road providing lots of places to hide.

It was past noon, and it seemed that we were getting nowhere. Everything looked the same. The ground was dry and rough, which made the wagon bounce around, and we all needed a rest.

Papa said, "Let's stop here and rest." We were ready for those words, and ready for lunch in the shade of the big cottonwood tree near the small creek. It felt cool and damp there by this small stream of water. Papa unhitched the team and took them and Barney down to get a refreshing drink. We also ate the snacks Mama had prepared at breakfast and we always drank plenty of water every time we stopped.

While we ate Papa was still puzzled. He said, "I know there is another road out here somewhere. When I came through here to buy our house I found a fairly good road, a traveled road soon after I left the cattle trail and we must have somehow missed it."

"Will, are you looking for any particular thing like a landmark that you remember?" Mama asked.

"No, I don't remember any landmarks like a big sand rock boulder or tree, but this just doesn't look the same to me. Maybe, we have not gone far enough yet. This loaded wagon with the team moves much slower than riding a horse."

We ate and rested awhile, then started rolling again, when over the next hill we saw four riders coming our way.

"Papa, look! Indians!" Sidney said crouching down peeping over the wagon top.

"Maybe they don't want us on their land." I said to Papa.

"No, it's just some men probably coming home from a hunt." Papa volunteered.

"I'm scared!" I told Mama.

She patted my shoulder and said, "Don't worry. Just listen."

When they reached us they stopped to talk. Their skins were really dark, but they looked friendly when they spoke in broken English to Papa. They had several wild turkeys tied to their horses. Papa told them we were looking for the main road through here going west, and they pointed him in the right direction. They nodded and rode on passed.

Sidney and I watched until they were almost out of sight, then Sidney said, "Boy, they were nice, and did you see their big, brown eyes?"

Papa said, "See, I told you they didn't care for us crossing their land."

Mama said, "Sidney, you are right. They were nice, and they did have pretty brown eyes."

I said, "Grandpa and Papa both have brown eyes like that; I wish I had dark brown eyes like theirs."

Sidney asked, "Are my eyes brown?"

"No, our eyes are much lighter than Papa's." I answered. "We have light colored eyes like Mama's."

Papa turned the wagon a little more north and we traveled on our way. Again, I saw a quick movement on the right side of the wagon in some tall grass, but I didn't say a word to anyone, but Sidney noticed my reaction.

"What did you see, Rhody?"

"I thought I saw something move back there behind those bushes."

Putting my hand to my lips, "Sh-hh, I just thought I saw something."

About that time Papa pointed and said, "Look, there's the road I'm looking for going west. This will be a much better ride from here on, and I know up this way somewhere I remember a Trading Post."

Sidney's eyes shined, "The Indians helped us, didn't they? You know Papa, you are right about everything. They are real nice people"

Papa laughed and said, "Well, before we go much further, let's stop along here under the next good shade and rest from that rough ride we've been on."

Mama said, "That's a good idea." We all agreed and soon found a good place where Sidney and I could run and jump around and exercise our legs awhile.

Lost in a Box

While running about avoiding thorns and nettles, Sidney ran smack into me. I yelled, "Sidney! "Watch out! Everywhere I turn you're right at my heels."

"Well, Rhody, I didn't mean to bump into you. Why did you stop like that anyway?"

"Look!" I said, pointing at some rocks near a clump of tall grass. "Look, there's a little box."

"I wonder what's in it?" Sidney asked. "Rhody, remember about snakes in the grass."

"Yeah, I remember. I'll look for snakes, and then I'll grab it real quick. It looks like it's tied with a faded ribbon." Sidney moved over, and I snatched the box out of the grass and shook it. "Yeah, there is something in it, but it won't open. It's rusty and stuck tight."

"Here, let me try." Sidney grabbed it and shook it real hard, and then I took it back from him. He said, "Well, maybe you can open it then."

"But Sidney, I feel strange opening something that's not mine."

"Shucks, Rhody it's yours now. You don't see anyone else around, do you? Hey, maybe it's a cowboy's candy box."

"Aw, don't be silly, Sidney. Cowboys don't tie ribbons on anything." I gave the lid a few whacks with a rock, rust flaked off in my hand and finally the box opened.

"What's in it?"

"A folder piece of paper, and . . ."

"Aw, that won't rattle. I heard something rattle!" Sidney interrupted.

"Oh, there's a lace collar and a letter, and look, Sidney, a golden locket on a chain. That's what we heard rattle – a locket!" Sidney grabbed for it again. "Stop, Sidney!" He watched me carefully open the locket. It unsnapped and looking back at me was the face of a little girl about my age. "Look, her hair is long, like mine, just darker."

"Yeah, she's pretty like you too." He handed it back, and I put the chain over my head, but quickly took it off.

"Rhody, can't you make up your mind? It looked pretty on you, its gold like your hair."

"Well, just knowing it belongs to someone else makes it kind of mysterious to me. I can't wear it. It isn't mine."

Papa called from the wagon. "What are you kids doing? You're too quiet. Come on, it's time to go now."

I ran to the wagon. "Look, Mama, look what I found!"

Mama took the locket, handling it carefully, and said, "Oh my, it's so pretty and looks like pure gold." I handed her the box and she looked at the beautifully tatted collar, and carefully handled the folded, yellowed letter from someone. "Oh my," she said, "this must be someone's treasure box. They must be mighty sad at losing it, especially this beautiful locket."

"But Mama she won't wear it." Sidney shared.

"Rhody, its okay for you to wear it, for there is no way to ever find the owner way out here."

"But, Mama, I can't wear it, it's not mine."

"Well, my knife is sure mine." Sidney bragged. "Papa, did you ever find anything on the trail like this? I found this knife and now Rhoda found a box of stuff."

"Well, as a matter of fact, I did, Son. See this watch of mine that I carry all the time, I found it in Oregon. I was riding Barney right through a town on a dirt main street, and it shined in the sun. I picked it up and could see that it was a good watch. After inquiring around while I stayed there, I never found any one to claim it, so I left town with it, and I've carried it all these years and it still keeps good time."

"See, Rhody, its okay to keep it for yours. I'm sure keepin' my knife."

Rhody jumped real quickly, "Papa, look! There in that brushy grass, I saw something move again." I stated for sure, "There is someone following us!"

"Rhody, we know, but it's just wild dogs or coyotes. I see movement myself once in a while. The land is full of them, so just relax now and enjoy the ride, for we are on the last long stretch of the road to our home. This road will soon lead us to where we turn north again and we will almost be at Uncle Jim's place."

"Papa, are we still in Indian Territory"

"Yes, all this land is Indian Territory, but this section of land here is known now as Oklahoma Territory. Norman, the town where we're going, is part of the land homesteaded by people who staked their claims as early as 1889 in the Land Runs. Each claim was for one hundred sixty acres."

"How did they know the land was theirs?"

"Each stake had a claim number, and when that person took their stake number to the Claims Office in Norman it was recorded on the Court House records as theirs. They had to live on that claim for five years to be given a clear Title of Ownership, called a 'Deed' to the land."

"Well, do we have a Title of Ownership to our land here?"

"Yes, Rhody, we have a deed to the land." Papa went on to explain that Mr. Rockford had lived on the land he claimed for almost ten years before he died. He had no sons, only two daughters who now live in other States, so Mrs. Rockford sold out to us. That's how we came to have one hundred sixty acres of good farm land. I paid Mrs. Redford and the land was deeded to us."

Sidney said, "Boy, I'll sure be glad to get there so I can see it and run and explore everywhere."

Papa said, "Well, you will have plenty of land to explore and plenty of chores to do too."

Sidney said, "Oh, I'll help you, Papa. I won't run away like Joel Ray did."

Mama said, "It will be so nice to have neighbors again, a school and a church family, and know many of the town's people."

On down the road we traveled visiting and planning what we wanted to do when we reached our new home. I opened and closed the little tin box over and over wondering about the face in the locket, and hoping to see her real soon.

Old Jake

I still kept getting glimpses of our traveling companion, but seldom said anything, for Papa was so sure it was wild dogs or coyotes. I was not convinced though. I secretly believed we had a prairie guardian watching over us, but I couldn't tell Sidney.

This trip was fun, but Sidney and I were especially ready for it to end. Mama too, for I don't think she had been feeling well. She was just tired riding on these bumpy roads, and I do believe my knees had calluses from riding with my knees on our padded quilt beside her.

There were always blackbirds sailing around, and as we watched the red dirt gullies along the road everywhere we also saw lots of crows who seemed very curious about us. They'd fly from tree to tree with us. I think it was the moving wagon that fascinated them. There were lots of other birds, and occasionally we saw a bird with a long tail like scissors that we'd never seen before. We called it the scissor bird. They moved fast. We also saw more horseback riders on this road that stopped to visit, and we enjoyed their visits too. One rider told us that we're not far from the Trading Post that Papa had mentioned earlier.

Sidney squealed at that news and I was ready too. Mama said she needs to buy sugar. Every time we pass wild berries, grapes or sand plums, we pick them, for that means a pudding or a cobbler.

Mama commented, "This land is rich in many good natural things like berries, wild grapes and plums, but it's hot as 'blue blazes' this time of year. I'm hoping for a good orchard at our new home, so we'll have lots of fruit like apples, pears, and peaches."

Papa said, "It has an orchard, but I didn't look it over very well. We can always plant more fruit trees."

Much of the time Sidney entertained himself shuffling around in his box of collected stuff, which he called his cowboy treasures, or whittling on something with his pocket knife he'd found on the trail. Mama and I chit-chatted together about things we'll do when we get to our new home, but sometimes, I just get plain bored. We had just gone around a slight bend and through a rugged gully, when I shouted, "Look! Sidney, outlaws are chasing us!"

Sidney ducked under Papa's legs like a scared rabbit. Papa looked quickly, then scolded me sternly, for that today he had no patience with my pranks. The horses were pulling hard through the rough terrain, and the old covered wagon jerked from side to side. That was about all he could handle at one time. I found out it was not a good time for my foolishness.

"Papa, I promise I won't upset Sidney anymore."

With saintly patience, Mama placed her hand on my shoulder. She didn't have to say a word. I knew what she meant, no more of that!

Mama touched Sidney and said, "Rhody was just kidding. Just think of all the good cowboys, Indians and families like us, who have traveled on these trails, just like we're doing now."

Papa said, "Yeah, many Indians, trappers, traders, and even preachers have passed this way through the years."

Sidney relaxed and said, "Yeah, remember the old man we saw back on the cattle trail in Texas with pots and pans hanging and clanging all over his wagon. Boy, he couldn't sneak up on anybody." We all laughed.

Papa said, "Just close your eyes now, and you can almost see and hear the tired, dusty cowboys riding herd on their cattle through areas like this. In fact the well known Jesse Chisholm Cattle Trail moving Texas Longhorns came right through this area, and think of all the Indians who have roamed this land in buffalo hunting parties looking for the herds. They used the buffalo for food and hides for their clothing and shelter."

"Oh, if these old prairies could talk, they would have lots of stories to tell." Mama reminded us.

Sidney said, "Yeah, even that cowboy who lost his knife I found could probably tell us a few tales too. Papa, now that we're passed that rough ground back there, would you tell us a story?"

"Have I told you about the time I was in Colorado and followed two old miners to their gold mine?"

"No, Papa. Tell us that one."

He started, "Well those Rocky Mountains are the most beautiful and interesting of any mountains I'd ever seen. More surprising than their beauty was the location of the mine shaft openings. Finding gold way up there always intrigued me. I wondered how they got their equipment and supplies up there. Well, I found out. Burros are strong and they can climb almost anything. They can climb where horses can't go."

"Was Barney with you?"

"Oh, yes. Barney went everywhere with me."

Papa stopped talking and said, "Jane, I believe this is the Trading Post I saw when I rode up here to buy the place. I'm remembering it now. Hey, Kids, you will get to stretch your legs here. You'll enjoy this. It is different than anything we've seen in a while. I'll finish my story later."

Sure enough a little further we got sight of Johnson's Trading Post and it looked like a small settlement. There were a few other people around too. This was exciting! Papa drove under a big shady tree and tied up the horses where they had a horse watering tank. The team and Barney were ready to drink and rest too. Papa helped Mama down, then Sidney and I jumped out of the wagon and walked toward the store building. There were some smaller outbuildings behind. Mama went on inside to look around and buy sugar, and told Sidney and I to stay around close. I intended to go in with Mama, but Sidney grabbed my arm and said, "Rhody, look!"

In the shade of the building near the door sat three old men on wooden benches talking and whittling. They nodded and one said, "Howdy, Folks," then went right on whittling. His knife caught Sidney's eye. Sidney watched him awhile and then wanted to walk closer, but stood back.

"Rhody, go over there with me. Will you? I want to see his pocket knife."

"Aw, you go on over there yourself. Don't be a 'fraidy-cat.' I'm going on in and look around with Mama."

"Please, Rhody."

We sauntered closer to the men, and I asked if my little brother could watch awhile. He wants to see your knives.

"Sure, Sonny, come on over here."

Sidney asked, "What'ch makin'?"

"I'll show you. I'm makin' a whistle. If you had a knife like mine you could make yourself a whistle like this one."

"Oh, I have a knife." Sidney said, and he whipped it out of his pocket and showed it to the old man.

"Well now, first, you've got to have the right kind of wood. Willow is best for whistles, because it hollows out easier and the wood is soft. That's the hardest part. Then you are ready to cut the notches for sound." He patiently showed Sidney each step, then he stopped and remarked. "Say Sonny, that's a fine lookin' knife you got there." He looked again at the knife and asked, "Where did you get this knife?"

"Oh, I found it on the trail." Sidney proudly said. "Papa says it is a real good knife too."

"Well, it is that for sure, a real good one. One of the best I've seen." He held it out for the other two to see. "Take a look." They each examined it closely.

One said, "Why I think the kid's found Jake's knife."

"Where is Mr. Jake now?" Sidney quickly asked.

"Well, Son, old Jake is not here anymore."

"Do you know where he lives?" Rhody asked.

"Yeah, I know. Old Jake was a cowpoke through and through, and was too old to go on that last cattle drive, but no one could talk him out of it."

"Son," the other man spoke up. "Old Jake is dead. Yeah, he died on that last Texas cattle drive. It was too much for him. I guess he lost that knife somewhere in Texas."

"Yeah, I found this one in Texas." We saw a lot of graves on the trail too. One of them could have been Old Jake." Sidney lowered his eyes and stood there timidly, not knowing what else to say.

The man who instructed Sidney how to make a whistle quickly said, "Well, Sonny, you know what? I think Old Jake would be mighty happy that you found his knife. He was very proud of it, and I see that you are too. Take good care of it for he sure paid a 'pretty penny' for it."

Sidney grinning from ear to ear said, "I sure will. I'll take good care of Old Jake's knife."

While I went on inside with Mama, Sidney ran to tell Papa that he visited with the old men and heard the story of Old Jake. He proudly said, "This is Old Jake's knife that I found." Papa went over and talked to them, and they told him the same story.

Mama bought the sugar, and she and I looked around in the store. It was an interesting place, and as we walked toward the door the couple followed us. They seemed happy to have someone new to visit with them. I showed them the picture in the locket I had in my dress pocket and asked, "Do you ever remember seeing this little girl in your store?"

They both looked, but shook their heads. The woman said, "The families usually have children, but I can't say that I remember her. She is a very pretty little girl."

Papa and Sidney came in about that time, so we thanked the couple, and as we drove away, I saw a shadow dart through the weeds across the road, but I didn't say anything. Sidney waved goodbye to the old men sitting in the shade.

Papa said, "Now they have something to talk about for awhile, the kid that found Old Jake's knife."

Sidney sat content with a peppermint stick in his hand and a new whistle in his pocket. He pulled out his knife and said, "Old Jake paid a 'pretty penny' for this, and I'm going to take real good care of it for him."

We drove on down the road again, all rested and refreshed, ready for Papa to finish his story.

Old Miners

We drove on awhile discussing the Trading Post experience, until we found a good camping place for the night. Traveling was getting easier and a lot more comfortable for the road was more traveled. They told Papa at the Trading Post that we're getting close to the Oklahoma Territory line. Each turn of the wheels brought us closer to our destination. We relaxed a little knowing we would soon be entering the land of the homesteaders in the Oklahoma Territory.

Papa explained that the homesteaders' land was land left over after the Indian land assignments to the Five Civilized Tribes were made by the Government. There were millions of acres left over, and that land was opened to white settlers in one hundred sixty acres farm sites. These Land Runs started as early as 1889, and after several land-runs the land was filled with farmers and ranchers.

"Papa, do we have to homestead the land?" Rhody asked.

"No, as I told you earlier, Mr. Redford home-steaded the land, and it was his to sell. It is ours now and it's ready for us to move onto as our own."

Sidney reminded Papa, "Don't forget to finish the story now."

Papa suggested, "It won't be long until we make camp, so let's wait until after we eat and help Mama clean up everything.

We soon found a shady campsite and it was getting cooler, so after we ate we all sat on a quilt ready for Papa's story. He stretched out to rest on his back, and Mama leaned over close to him. Sidney and I sat with our knees drawn up under our chins. We were all-ears, for Papa and Mama both told good stories.

"Well," Papa started, "as I said I was in this little Colorado town looking for work, when I spotted these two old, loud-mouthed miners laughing and talking with friends. I listened closely and overheard them say they were leaving the next morning with supplies, and would probably be gone about three months. They disappeared before I got to talk to them, so I decided to just follow them the next morning. I was curious about mining and thought this might be a good job for the next three months. I was young and inexperienced, so I set out to follow them."

"Did they know you were following them?"

"Oh, no. That's the reason I followed them at a distance. I had not said anything to them. They didn't know me. I really wanted to try out mining, for all I'd done up to that time was work as a ranch hand to make money for myself."

"Didn't they see you following?"

"No, I stayed back from them. They'd go out of sight, and then I'd see them again. As I followed, I didn't realize at first that we were climbing higher. They kept moving on and so did Barney and I. It got more rocky and rugged. Right off I saw that it was going to be a rough climb for Barney, so I walked most of the way and helped him over the rough spots. The trail was getting too steep for Barney, and he was getting too tired and skittish. Horses are not made for climbing like burros, so I knew we could not go much further. About the time I thought we could not go any further, we came across a little mountain meadow with a small lake. I stood in awe of its beauty, for I came from flat farm land, and had no idea there were meadows and lakes in the mountains. I became so distracted by all this, that I lost sight of the miners. They quickly disappeared. Their trail just vanished. Poof! They were gone. Well, it was almost sundown, so I decided Barney and I would bed-down here for the night, and look for the miners in the morning."

"Papa, were you afraid all by yourself with Barney." I asked."

"Yeah, I felt a little uneasy, but I staked out Barney so he could enjoy the grass, made out my bedroll, ate a can of beans, and before I knew it, the sun dropped behind the mountain and it was the blackest dark and the coldest place I'd ever known. I laid there and watched the stars twinkle like they were just right close above. On the side of the mountain where we were climbing, I saw a tiny flicker of light way up there. I said to myself, now how in the world did they get up there so fast? I was so tired I dropped off to sleep thinking to myself I'll find them tomorrow.

"Did you go to sleep right then, Papa," Sidney asked.

"Yeah, I did. I was so tired, and I even slept through the sunrise. When I opened my eyes to the warm sunshine, I already had a guest standing there."

"One of the old miners stood over me holding a shot gun to my belly."

"A gun!" We gasped.

"Hey," he yelled, "Wake up, Sonny! What'ch want anyway? What'ch you follern' us fer?"

"Just lookin' for a job, Sir." I quickly answered. I had never looked down the barrel of a shotgun before, so this farm boy from Missouri quickly explained. I told them I needed a job, and wanted to see them about learning to work in the mine with them."

The old miner spoke short and he meant it, "Well, this ain't the way to do it, Sonny. Now git packed and be on your way back down the trail. We ain't got no job fer 'ya."

"Yes Sir!" I said. The old miner stood right there until I packed and started back down the way we came.

"I bet you hurried, didn't you, Papa?"

"I sure did, but I tell you getting off that mountain with Barney was worse than climbing up with him. So when we finally reached level ground, Barney and I stopped to rest, then hurried on into town to eat and then on to the Bar-J Ranch that I heard was hiring ranch hands."

"Did you get a job?"

"Sure did! I was glad to be there."

"Papa, I liked that story. Did you go on to Oregon from Colorado?" I asked, for I'd heard him talk about Oregon too.

"Yes, later on, and that is a pretty place too, but that will have to be another story at another time. Let's get to bed now, so we can get an early start in the coolness of the morning, I think tomorrow we'll be getting to the railhead at Purcell."

"Will we see a train at Purcell?" Sidney asked.

"I hope so, Son. The great Atchison, Topeka and Santa Fe train comes through here on a regular basis picking up cattle."

Papa, will we see lots of cattle there?" I asked

"Oh, I'm sure we will for cattle are held there for the next shipment. We won't tarry long though, for that is where we go north on our last stretch of road. In a couple of days or so we will find Jim's grocery store in Norman, then just a few miles further is our home waiting!"

Mama said, "Home! Oh, that sounds so good to me. Home is a wonderful word!"

Birthday Surprise

The next morning Papa announced first thing, "Today is August 5th and Rhody's birthday, so this will be a grand day for us."

"Yeah, Rhody, since this is your birthday, let's not look for your spooky old shadow today, even if he is our prairie guardian, let's give him a rest," then Sidney announced, "Rhody has looked behind every bush and rock ever since we got into Indian Territory."

Everyone laughed and Sidney said, "So why don't you wear your golden locket today to celebrate your birthday."

"No, Sidney, I'm saving that for the little girl when I find her."

Mama said, "Happy Birthday, Rhody, on birthday number twelve." Everyone wished me a happy birthday and gave me a big hug, even Sidney.

Sidney said, "I wish you would wear your locket today on your birthday . . . just for me!"

"No, Sidney, I don't want to wear the locket!"

Even though it was my birthday, this day was no difference. We rode on hour after hour, each in our own thoughts, except Sidney. He thinks out loud. We stopped and picked plums so Mama could make us a plum pudding. Papa let us ride Barney too, since the road was smooth and well traveled and because it was my birthday. We always enjoy Barney, and he enjoys us too, for he lopes along ahead of the wagon carrying us from one shade to the other. There were tall cottonwood shade trees everywhere. Papa let us ride over closer to the willows too, but not near the river water, and of course, we were all eyes watching for wild dogs. I secretly watched for our prairie guardian, but today I never saw a shadow anywhere. I didn't even mention it, since we agreed not to talk about it. Riding Barney was always fun and a real birthday treat for me and Sidney.

Late afternoon we camped in a nice shady area to get out of the summer heat. Mama fired up the Dutch oven to bake biscuits or cornbread. I didn't suspect that she was baking a cake until it began to smell sweet.

Sidney squealed, "Rhody, we're having birthday cake!"

Mama said, "It won't be light and fluffy without eggs, but it will be good with sugared plums."

Papa came and sat in the shade with us and asked. "What is this? Do I smell birthday cake?" We ate our supper, then Mama cut the birthday cake. Sidney insisted on lighting a small stick for me to blow out. "Wait, let me make a wish." I gave it a big puff and out went the flame. They sang happy birthday to me. I told them, "I will always remember this special day, my twelfth birthday."

Sidney asked, "Rhody, what did you wish for? I bet I know." He giggled. "I bet you wished to see Joel Ray again."

"Well, I just may see him again someday. Who knows?" Papa had saved back some peppermint sticks, one for each of us, and Mama had bought me blue hair ribbons at the Trading Post for my braids and saved them for my birthday. Sidney gave me his lucky rabbit's foot, but I asked him to carry it for me, since I did not always have a pocket.

He agreed and said, "We'll share the good luck."

My day was special. That night around the campfire we heard a howling sound from over the way. "Papa, do you think that could be our guardian angel?"

"No, Rhody, it's just a wolf howling over there somewhere. They feast on rabbits and small game. They sound lonesome, but they have lots of company. They run in family packs."

I said, "Good night, I will always remember this special birthday while on the trail to our new home." I laid my head on the pillow that night and quickly went to sleep to dream of meeting the little girl in the locket as birthday sugarplums danced in my head.

The Revelation

Papa announced the next morning that we're just about a two day's drive from our new home. Now, those were exciting words to all of us. Nearing the bridge on the road running close to the South Canadian River low lands, he explained that all through this area were wet boggy places and sink holes.

I asked, "What's a sink hole?"

"Well, it's always in marshy land in places that don't dry up, like it has water under it and stays wet all the time. It's just part of the underground water from the river. They are dangerous for a horse or other big animals. They have to be pulled out."

"Is it like quick sand?" Mama asked.

"It's kind'a like quick sand, but is not deep like quick sand. You can only sink so far, but is very difficult to get out without help. We must avoid these wet swampy places, but those places are closer to the river bed. We don't need to worry, for this road is too far out from the river."

We stopped awhile to rest and Papa let Sidney and I run around, for it was fun in the sandy soil. We ran on ahead and our interests took us out through the willows. As usual Sidney scooted on ahead kicking up rocks, and scampering about in the sunshine, as I day dreamed of our new home and friends. Papa said we will be home real soon, so I walked and daydreamed of what it will be like to have a home again and friends at school and friends living by us on nearby farms. I thought I might even find the little girl in the locket living near us, for I found it on this road back there somewhere. She just might live here too.

Suddenly, I looked around and Sidney was out of my sight and yelling, "Rhod-e-e-e!"

I just knew he had run into a pack of wild dogs or been bitten by a snake. I couldn't see him, but I heard him.

"Rhod-e-e-e, hurry! Call Papa. I'm in the mud!"

I heard fear and panic in his voice, and when I saw him he was struggling frantically near some muddy brush and weeds. I screamed for Papa, for I knew my brother was in that muddy marsh. I had to get him out. I tried to reach him! "Sidney, why did you go way out here anyway?" I screamed at him, "Didn't you hear what Papa said about sink holes?"

He gasps, "I forgot! I saw some pretty flowers over there and wanted to pick them for Mama."

I was afraid to walk out there too far, so I got down and crawled closer to reach his hand, but still couldn't reach him. I grabbed an old broken tree limb and held it out to him. Demanding, "Sidney, grab it. Hold on tight. No, don't jerk, you're pulling me in too." All the while I was yelling, "Papa! Hurry, Papa!"

I panicked when I heard a dog barking wildly, I thought of dogs, a pack of wild dogs, when about that time Papa grabbed onto my dress, and pulled hard. I turned to look, but it was not Papa! It was the golden dog pulling my dress held tightly in his mouth trying to back up.

Papa and Mama had heard our screams and were startled by the sound of a dog barking. They both ran toward us just in time to see the golden dog bolt from behind his cloak of bushes and rush like a soldier charging on command to help us. Papa took hold of the tree limb and helped the dog pull us out. We were both safe, but half scared to death. We were a muddy mess. The golden dog stood off to the side wagging his tail.

"See, Papa, I told you our guardian angel left his dog for us. He's followed us all the way. I just knew that was him that I kept seeing. I just knew it was him!"

"Well, Rhody, from the looks of it, you were right." Papa laughed.

Mama laughed too for she saw the golden dog bolt to the rescue. She said, "He barked like Gabriel blowing his horn when he came out from hiding."

The guardian dog walked gently into my muddy, outstretched arms wagging his tail and barking, as if to say, "I've guarded you all across this prairie. Now, take me home with you." After bath time in the river, we climbed aboard the wagon to continue our journey.

The golden dog hesitated, until Papa turned and motioned, "Come on, you're gonna' ride too."

"What shall we name him?" I asked. "We can't keep calling him golden dog or the Indian's dog."

Mama said, "Let's name him Gabriel. He reminded me of God's guardian angel flying into action."

That day he became a loyal member of our family, and we called him Gabe for short. He hunted rabbits, romped with us, and enjoyed riding in the wagon at times. One day with my arm around Gabe, I said, "Gabe, I wish you could talk and tell us stories about you and your old Indian friend. I'd sure like to hear that story."

Papa laughed and patted Gabe on the head as if they shared a secret. Papa said, "The old Indian may have been our prairie guardian angel that night at the campsite, but I still think he was just a tired, old Indian Warrior, who found a new home for his faithful dog. Isn't that right, Gabe?" Gabe barked and wagged his tail, as if he understood.

Gabe settled down by my side as if that was his place. He looked at me with his big, brown eyes and listened intently as I told him the story of the lost locket and the little girl's face I hoped to find someday. Our covered wagon creaked on slowly carrying us closer and closer by the hour to our new home in the land of settlers.

Papa said excitedly, "Now stay alert for we're getting close and watch for we are just a few miles from Jim's Grocery Store."

Sidney asked, "Do you think he'll have some peppermint sticks?"

Papa laughed with all of us and said, "Oh, Son, I'm sure he will! Grocery stores always have peppermint sticks."

Home at Last

Those last few miles riding along together, Sidney and I sat huddled close with Gabe near Mama's feet on the old quilt. Gabe liked to lie close and watch us with his big brown eyes. I wish I could read his thoughts. He had walked many miles following us on the old rugged Indian trail, so now he enjoyed a welcome ride in the wagon with us. He hopped off occasionally to chase a rabbit, but otherwise stayed close. Each time he ran out of sight I wanted to call him back, for I was afraid he'd leave and go back to the old Indian.

Papa reassured me, "Don't worry. He's at home with us now, or he wouldn't have followed us in the first place. I know his old Indian friend encouraged him to come for he was old and knew he would probably die soon, so he wanted his dog to have a good home and family."

I sat with my arm around Gabe just daydreaming of meeting the little girl in the locket. I often took the locket out of its box to just look at it, for it truly was a pretty gold locket. "Mama, isn't this locket pretty? I have great hopes of meeting this little girl real soon."

Mama said, "Rhody, I hope you find her too, but it will be a miracle if you ever find her here."

Somehow, today the sun seemed brighter and hotter, but we didn't seem to mind, for we're so filled with anticipation of seeing our home today. Gabe and I sat close together just watching the blue skies full of fluffy white summer clouds floating about like great wads of cotton; dusty wildflowers and weeds bow to us in the quiet breeze as the wagon slowly moved along.

Mama commented, "I'm so thankful that we didn't have to endure any summer storms on our way. We could have used some rain and coolness along the way, but not summer storms."

"Jane, you're so right about that." Papa said. "Heavy rains would have slowed us down for days.

I'm so ready to get settled in our new life here. Just think, we'll be at Jim's store this morning, and then it's just a few miles away to our own place."

We shivered with excitement. "After weeks of traveling with all our adventures, and followed by our unknown guardian dog, we are so ready to be home and settled again." Mama said.

As we crossed the bridge over the Canadian River we heard excitement in Papa's voice. He shouted, "We're almost here! Look at the northern horizon. Look! You can see it right over there, pointing to the little town of Norman! In a few more miles we'll be there on Main Street right in front of Jim's Grocery."

We were filled with expectation as we rolled closer and closer into this little town, a place we'd never seen before and will now be our home town. Our eyes missed nothing, as Papa stated, "We will never forget this day!"

"What's that big building over there, Papa?"

"That's the University of Oklahoma, established in 1889."

Mama was impressed. "I never expected that!"

We drove through the narrow, dusty streets where people lived, then further north to the main part of town. The bank building sign also read "Established 1889." Papa told us that all these businesses were first started over night in tents during the land runs, and even many of the homesteaders lived in tents and sod houses or dugouts until their houses could be built later for shelter. The first land run was in November, so many of them endured the entire winter in those makeshift homes. They had to be determined, hard working people. As we drove, Papa talked fast, trying to tell us all he knew about the town. He proudly pointed to a schoolhouse, and all the friendly townspeople and kids out playing waved to us as we slowly drove passed.

My eyes were busy searching every face for that little girl. Mama smiled as we passed a church.

Sidney teased, "Rhody, are you looking for the girl in the locket or for Joel Ray?"

"Oh, Sidney, quit talking about the locket and Joel Ray. I will find the little girl someday, you just watch, and you know Joel Ray lives in Texas. I'm not apt to find him here now. He went back home."

We drove down the wide Main Street to Uncle Jim's nice little grocery store on the north side of the street. We parked in the wagon-yard behind the store under shady trees; Papa tied the team to wait until we got back. We all walked into the store and when Uncle Jim saw us, he shouted, "You made it!" He grabbed Papa and they hugged and looked at each other and hugged again. It had been several years since they had seen each other. Uncle Jim hugged Mama and said, "Jane, you're just as pretty as ever," then he hugged me and kissed my cheek, and patted Sidney on the head.

Uncle Jim looked a lot like Papa, just a little older, I guess. He asked all about the folks in Texas and Papa gave him an update on everyone.

Papa asked, "Jim, how's Ruth and the two boys? Kids grow up so fast; I know they are good-sized boys by now."

"Oh, Ruth is fine, and that James is taller than I am, and William, your namesake, is growing fast like Sidney. James wants to go to the University. I hope I can afford that, for he really wants to be a lawyer. I think he would make a good one."

Papa agreed, "Yes, I remember he always was a smart one and quite a talker. Sure beats what we did, doesn't it? We never saw the inside of a school after the eighth grade." They both laughed together.

Uncle Jim said, "Well, now Will, with that in mind just remember when Rhody and Sidney finish the eighth grade out there at Pleasant Hill School, they can always stay here with us through the week to finish their education here at Norman."

"Jim, we'll sure take you up on that offer when the time comes," said Papa.

He invited us to stay a few days with them and rest up a little, but Papa said, "Thanks, Jim, but we're too close to home to stop now. We're just a few miles away, so we'll go on and if you see John before we do, tell him we're here, and we'll see them in a few days. We're anxious to go on now, get settled and get rested in our own home. It's been a long trip for us."

Uncle Jim replied, "Will, I understand that. Do you need any supplies today?"

Mama spoke up, "Jim, I think we're good for a few days. I'll make a full list and we'll be back soon to stock up on everything."

Papa said, "Thanks, Jim. I guess we have everything we need today; except for maybe a bag of peppermint sticks."

We all laughed and Jim said, "Oh, I've got them already bagged and ready to go. Sidney can carry them."

We walked back to the wagon, as Uncle Jim was saying, "I'll tell John that you're here. He may be in town tomorrow. He and Mandy live just a few miles south from here, but he knows you bought the Redford place, so he'll be over. Will, you sure got yourself a nice place there."

Papa replied, "Yeah, Mrs. Redford was sure good to us, for she left everything in the house for us except her organ, her grandfather clock and her sewing machine, so we're pretty well fixed-up for now. We didn't have to move any furniture at all. After we get there we can see what else we might need."

"Will, I'm sure happy you and your family are here safely. We prayed for you all the way," said Uncle Jim.

Mama said, "Thanks, for God truly did take good care of us. It was like an adventure and we'll share it all with you soon."

Before we drove away I got out the locket and showed it to Uncle Jim. I told him I had found it along the way, and wondered if he happened to know this little girl.

He said, "No, can't say that I do, but the boys might know her. You'll have to show it to them."

We drove away waving, when Sidney asked first thing, "Papa, where's our house from here?"

Pointing northeast, Papa answered, "A few miles that way." We drove on our way out of town. We went east a mile and from there, we turned north.

My eyes continually searched each face we passed. I said, "Mama, I really hope that little girl lives here. She'll be my best friend. I just know I'll find her here somewhere."

"Well, Rhody, I'm not so sure of that, for this main road goes on north, or they could have turned off the trail anywhere back there. Besides, she may not even be a little girl any longer, for we don't know how old that picture might be."

"Yeah, Rhody, she may not live here, so why don't you put on your pretty locket and wear it home to celebrate."

"No, Sidney, I've told you I'm not wearing it. It belongs to someone else! I'll find her someday. Oh, I may even see her at school when it starts."

"Well, I think you ought to wear it. It would look so pretty with your hair. I sure like my knife and I use it all the time."

We drove north then Papa said, "Look, here's your school house on the corner!" A nice little white two-roomed school called Pleasant Hill with swings and a big yard, and a big storm shelter for summer storms.

We stopped to look it over and let the team rest. At the school house corner it was only a short distance to the Little River Bridge. The crossing was a shady, quiet area that made you want to listen to the strange sound of the dark, moving water below. Papa said our home was less than a mile on down the road.

Papa warned, "Now keep your eyes opened for just passed the four-corners our house will come up next." We slowly drove on. Papa started pointing, "Look, pointing to the right, see it? There it is on the hill! We are here!"

"Look, Rhody! There's our house." Sidney shouted.

We drove up our driveway to the house on the hill at Route three, Norman, O.T. Mama smiled as she saw pink roses climbing on the south fence up to the house. Papa was real quiet, as he watched our eyes feast on all we saw. We came to a stop between the house and the windmill.

Papa said, "Whoa!" I suddenly remembered that day when he said Giddy-up weeks ago when we first started our journey in Texas. Papa jumped to the ground and shouted, "We're home!" We all sat still a minute and just looked at the house, the windmill, the barn, the trees, and the yard.

Mama exclaimed, "Oh, Will, it is a fine place just like you said, and it has a nice porch too. Oh, we're home at last!" Tears streamed down her sweet, tired face.

Sidney and I hopped off of the wagon, Gabe jumped off too. Papa lifted Mama to the ground, hugged her and said, "Welcome home, Jane."

Sidney said in surprise, "Papa, this is a real house, just like you said."

"Yeah, I told you all about it; it is a good house, a big barn, a windmill, and acres of good land. A dream comes true for us!" He hugged Mama again and said proudly. "Jane, look, you even have some window boxes for flowers."

We all felt 'at home' the minute we walked inside. Mama exclaimed, "Oh, Will, it's just as you described it in every detail. This is a wonderful house for us."

Papa motioned for us to join hands in a circle and Papa said, "Lord, we are thankful for our safe journey to our new home. Bless this house and land, and each person who lives here, and each guest who enters these doors. May peace and contentment abide here with us forever. Amen."

First thing, Sidney and I claimed our bedrooms, while Mama looked over the kitchen.

Papa said, "Okay, kids, look around quickly, then come on for we've got lots of unloading to do. Sidney, you bring in some fire wood for the kitchen stove, so Mama can cook our supper. Rhody, bring in Mama's cooking pans and whatever she needs to cook. Sidney, I'll help you pump water from the windmill. While you all are busy with all that, I'll take the team and Barney on to the barn to water and feed and get them brushed down, so they can settle in for the night. We will unload the rest of the wagon tomorrow."

After all that was done, we ate our supper and relaxed as we visited awhile seated around the table.

Gabe explored the place and settled in quietly on the porch by the door. We were all bone tired from traveling so long, and our first night at home in our own beds truly was a time to remember.

Our New Life

It was in August when we arrived at our new home, and we knew school would start soon. We were ready and anxious to meet our new friends and neighbors. I was sure this is where I'd find my little friend in the locket.

Some of the nearby farm families came over right away to visit and get to know us. They all invited us to church and made us feel very welcome. We met their children of all ages, and enjoyed all of them, for they will be our new school friends. We were excited, but I did not see that special face. The men folk talked farming, planting, and tools, while Mama enjoyed hearing about the latest plans of the community women. They were all exceptionally friendly, as most country neighbors are. They spoke highly of the Redfords and had hoped for a family like us to move on this farm place. They mentioned to us about the Fall Festival soon, a community gathering held each year before school starts. We made plans to attend and meet many other neighbors right away.

Uncle John and Aunt Mandy came to visit in a day or two and bought lunch with them; Aunt Mandy said she knew we would not be ready for company yet.

Mama said, "Oh, Mandy, you should not have done that, but thanks. I know it will be delicious, for I remember your cooking."

Uncle John and Papa never stopped talking. They had so much catching up and sharing to do. Sidney and I thoroughly enjoyed our cousins, Verl Anne and Wayne. Verl Anne was about my age and she had light colored hair too. Wayne was ten years old, but they attended a different school. We had fun playing together all afternoon. It was good to know we had some real family living so close like we had in Texas.

The first Sunday we attended Sunday School and church, and of course, my eyes searched every face there. Everywhere we went I never quit searching, for I knew one of these days, I'd find that face.

Sidney teased, "Rhody, you're just like an old U.S. Marshall looking for bad guys. You never give up! Are you ever going to wear that locket?"

"No, I'll just keep looking. She may even start to school with us here."

As the weeks passed the fall leaves changed to amber and red, still clinging tightly on the trees made the trees beautiful, especially the golden willows against the red clay ruts on the road. Tall cottonwood trees fluttered their bright yellow leaves like silent, tinkling bells, and the maples and Blackjack Oak trees soon turned brilliantly red. The Oak trees were loaded with acorns and squirrels frantically gathered for their winter food. Our pecans were also falling and ready to gather. Fall Festival time was here and big plans were in the works to celebrate on the school grounds.

I just knew this festival would be the place where I'd find the little girl; for many families would be there that we've not yet met. Mama and I planned what to bring. Everyone was to take enough food for their family and then it was all put together for all to eat. Mama made a list of supplies for Papa and

Sidney to buy when they went to Norman this morning. When they returned about five or six hours later, Sidney was full of talk in detail, and I do mean detail. We heard all about Uncle Jim's apron he wore at the store; how he cut meat, and added up real fast the amount we owed him. Sidney must have prowled the whole store, for he mentioned every little thing in detail.

He told me, "Rhody, I only saw two little girls in the store, and I looked at their faces real good, but maybe we'll see your little locket girl at the picnic tomorrow."

Early Saturday morning Mama and I started cooking. We got the stove real hot to bake two apple pies and I made a batch of sugar cookies. We fried chicken, made potato salad and deviled the eggs that a neighbor brought over to us yesterday.

It was a fun day and we met folks from everywhere. There were kids galore, big kids, little kids, babies, and all in-between. While I played and got acquainted I saw each face. All the girls about my age seemed to enjoy getting acquainted, and they liked my story about our Indian Guardian Angel and his dog. I told them I kept notes of the whole trip for I wanted to always remember it all.

One of the girls, Sarah Beth and I seemed to gravitate together, and found we didn't live too far apart. Sarah Beth wanted to see Gabe. We also found that we may be in the same grade at school, so I told Sarah Beth all about finding the locket and picture, and invited her to come over and see it sometimes. "You may even know her. It's a real pretty locket," I said.

"Do you wear it?" she asked.

"Oh, no, I don't feel it belongs to me." I answered."

Everyone at the picnic seemed to have fun. Sidney was in 'pig-heaven' with all those boys. The little kids were getting tired and babies were napping under shade trees on quilt pallets everywhere you looked.

I never saw Mama and Papa have so much fun getting acquainted, eating, laughing and listening in on little groups chatting here and there. At times men huddled in little groups under shade trees, while ladies cleaned up the picnic mess. It was a fun day, and by late afternoon everyone started loading up left-over food and their kids to go home. The school ground was totally cleaned before we left. We all had a few miles to go, and everybody had chores to do before dark, so we drove away waving to each other. We looked forward to getting better acquainted with all these families.

Riding home we all had stories to share about someone we'd met. "This was a good gathering," Papa said. "I really enjoyed meeting our neighbors. Most of the men-folk were interesting and helpful about crops and weather here. They told me about the livestock auction each Friday, so I'll go next Friday and buy us a couple of good milk cows and some pigs to feed. We gotta' have ham and bacon for breakfast."

Mama said, "Lydia Jones, said they have a dozen laying hens we can buy. I told her we'd be over for them."

We all agreed we had fun. Sidney talked about Henry. He didn't know his last name, or who he belonged to, but said they had fun and shared knife stories. I shared with them about Sarah Beth Anders, who will be a class mate and I think they live close to us.

Papa remarked, "Yeah, I met a Bill Anders. They live about three miles from us. He's going to the auction with me Friday."

"I think Sarah Beth and I will be in the same grade. I told her about finding the locket. They all liked my story of the old Indian Guardian and his dog, and they want to meet Gabe."

Mama really liked the ladies too. She said, "They were all fun. I never laughed so much about nothing. We just enjoyed being together.

"I can't wait to see everyone again in the morning at church." I said. "I sure hope there are some other families to see if they have any little girls. So far, I've not seen anyone who even favors her face, and I've ask some of the kids if they have any other sisters at home."

Papa laughed, "Rhody, I declare you have the whole family looking for that face. Everywhere I go I find myself looking closely at each little face I see."

School Days

Sunday morning we attended church, and after going there a few weeks, I looked for any new families with little girls who might have the resemblance to the face in the locket. I have been disappointed again and again, so last Sunday I said as we rode home, "School tomorrow is the only place left to look, and we've probably already met all of them." I felt so discouraged.

Monday morning came and the start of school. Sidney and I were excited and could hardly wait to get there. I remarked about the bridge as we crossed over it in the wagon, saying, "I'd never before noticed those hollow sounds when we cross over it, but this morning it sounded spooky to me."

"Aw, Rhody, you are just excited." Sidney commented. "You'll get used to it when we walk across it two times every day."

Mama and Papa brought us to school early that first morning to meet our teachers and enroll us as new residents. We first met Mrs. Rollins who teaches grades one through five. She'll be Sidney's teacher this year, and then we met Mr. Rollins who teaches grades six through eight. I spoke up shyly to him, "I've never had a man-teacher before."

Mr. Rollins laughed, "Oh, I promise not to bite."

"Do you have any little girls?" I asked.

"No, Rhody, we have not been blessed with children, but we love teaching children." He turned to Papa and said "My wife and I work here as a team and live right here on the grounds in the house provided by the school district."

Mama and Papa visited a few minutes after enrolling us, then said goodbye. They seemed pleased with the teachers who had been here several years and were a part of the entire community. The teachers welcomed us kindly as newcomers.

We enjoyed our classmates that day and when school was out, we hurried on home after school.

That day I hardly noticed the bridge for two other kids walked with us to the four-corners where they turned west, while we went on straight a short ways. We hurried on down the road, then up our driveway racing through the door. I said, "Oh, yum, Mama, I smell sweet potatoes baking. It smells so good in here and I'm hungry."

Mama replied, "I've also baked some sugar cookies while I had the oven hot. How was school today?"

Sidney answered excitedly, "Mrs. Rollins is real nice, and I saw some of the same boys at the festival. We played marbles at recess, and Mrs. Rollins let me tell about finding Old Jake's knife on the trail and then meeting his friends at the Trading Post. Some of the other kids had things to tell too about their summer. She listened to some classes read out loud, while others silently read a history book to themselves."

"Oh, Mama, I got to see Sarah Beth again. She is in my grade and I met some other girls too, and they were all real nice to me. Sarah Beth has a big brother in the eighth grade named Brent. He's nice too. I've never known a Brent. I hope I can remember his name. But Mama, I did not see anyone who looked anything like the little girl. I'm really disappointed about that, for I was so sure she would be there today."

"Rhody, she may go to another school," Mama stated.

Sidney piped up, "Just wear the locket, Rhody, it belongs to you."

"I don't know what I'll do with the locket if I can't find her," I slowly replied. "I may just wear it next Sunday to church. At least that will please Sidney."

"Rhody, are you really going to wear your locket Sunday?" exclaimed Sidney.

"Now, Sidney, I said I might wear it."

Sunday morning came, and I wore my blue dress Mama had made for me and my blue birthday bows for my braids. I put the chain over my head, but just couldn't leave it. I quickly took it off, put the locket back in the tin box and pushed it back in the far corner of my closet, saying to myself, "It can just stay lost!"

I came out of my room to go, when Sidney opened his mouth to speak, but I held up my hand to stop him. "I decided not to wear it today after all."

"Aw, Rhody, I wish you'd give up on that face. You'll never find her here."

"Well, maybe not, but . . ."

Face in the Locket

The weeks and months passed slowly for me, because I felt sad about giving up on the idea of finding the little girl here. Though I enjoyed every day at school, and made good friends and found many I liked especially well. Sarah Beth became my best friend, and I liked her brother a lot. He was fun to be around and I think he liked me too.

Papa said this morning that if the weather is good on Saturday, he wants all of us to go to town together. Sidney's eyes shined, for a trip to town meant peppermint sticks. I was excited too, because Mama planned for us to shop for material to make a red Christmas dress for me.

She said, "The ladies mentioned at the Festival that the school always plans a big Christmas community program at school. I want you to be ready for it with a pretty red dress."

"Mama, I want a red ribbon for my hair for that night too, not bows on my braids."

Saturday morning came and I quickly dressed in my favorite yellow checked dress and yellow bows. Again I gave some thought to wearing the locket, but decided against it. Instead of putting it away I just dropped it in my skirt pocket. Deep down I guess I really had not given up on my search, for I thought I just might see her somewhere in a store or on the street with her family. What a wonderful surprise that would be for me!

Sidney was wound tight with excitement about going to town, and chattered all the way there. I do believe he could carry on a conversation with a fence post.

I asked him, "What are you buying today?"

"Oh, I'm looking for a blue marble. I've saved some money to buy one if I find the one I want," he said.

"Why blue?" I asked.

"Oh, a 'blue' makes good shots! Johnny Simpson beats me all the time with his."

He teased, "Are you looking for anything today, except the little girl's face?"

"I'm just shopping with Mama. We may buy some red material to make me a new Christmas Dress."

Sidney snarled a little, "Kind of early for Christmas, isn't it?"

"Well, it takes time, you know, to make a dress."

"Three months?" He questioned.

Papa spoke up, "Sidney, let it go."

When we arrived in town, Sidney went with Papa, and Mama and I shopped around and just looked at ready-made dresses for ideas, then we went to McCall's Dry Goods Store to look at material for my dress. We found just what we wanted. It will make a pretty Christmas dress! Mama had a list of things to buy for the kitchen too.

"Oh, look, Mama, we haven't been in Wagoner's General Store yet."

"Oh, that reminds me," Mama said, "that some of the ladies had mentioned that Mrs. Wagoner had been very ill, but was now back helping her husband in the store again. Let's go in and meet her, and I'll buy my kitchen items in there."

As we entered the store, there was a tall, slim woman with dark hair and dark eyes greeting us from behind the counter. I gasp at the sight of her! I grabbed Mama's hand. She looked a lot like the face in the locket! I whispered to Mama, "Look at her face!"

Smiling and walking toward us, the lady introduced herself as Jane Wagoner. Mama said, "Jane Wagoner, it's good to meet you. I'm Jane Lawson." Laughing, Mama said, "Our names should be easy enough for us to remember. This is my daughter Rhoda Lee, but we call her Rhody. We also have a nine year old son."

"Oh," she said, "we have a fourteen year old son. You'll meet him around here some time."

She and Mama chatted a few minutes, and I noticed her dark brown eyes often shifted to me as she talked with Mama. I watched her when she wasn't looking at me too. I became so distracted by her that I almost forgot why we went in there, but she helped Mama find the items she needed and then we went to the counter to pay.

She looked intently at me and stated, "So your name is Rhody."

"Yes, I'm Rhody and I just had my twelfth birthday."

I moved closer to Mama, and asked, "Do you have a little girl?"

"No, not here now," she hesitated. "She isn't here." She looked away as she talked softly.

Thinking that at last I'd found her, I quickly asked, "Where is she? What is her name:"

"Oh, her name is Martha Ruth." She said. "She died of pneumonia, soon after we moved here a few years ago. My folks all say she looked exactly like me. Martha was ten years old, and I still miss her so much."

Mama said, "Oh, we are so sorry."

I had to know, so I asked, "Do you have a picture of her?"

She lowered her eyes, "No, not anymore. Somewhere on the trail while moving here from Texas, I lost my locket with our only good picture of her after she was older. I have pictures of her growing up, but the last one taken was in my locket. I'll always remember her little face though and her beautiful dark hair and eyes."

As she went on telling Mama more about her little daughter, I reached my hand deep into the bottom of my skirt pocket, and felt the smoothness of the locket in my hand. I gripped it tightly. Mrs. Wagoner kept remembering. She said, "Each night I'd take off my locket and put it in a little tin box with Mother's lace collar and my brother's last letter. I don't know where or how it happened, but I lost that box. We searched all around our campsite, but never found it. I know it's gone forever and it makes me so sad since we had not taken a new picture of her after we moved here."

I squeezed Mama's hand, and she knew what I was thinking, but she didn't know I had the locket in my pocket. I slowly lifted the chain from my pocket with the locket dangling and asked, "Is this your locket?"

Mrs. Wagoner gasped, "Oh," she looked startled at the swinging gold locket. She quickly stepped closer. "Why yes, Rhody, it is! Where on earth did you find it?"

"I found the tin box in some tall grass on the trail moving here from Texas. I guess we must have camped in the same place. I've looked everywhere for the little girl in the picture. I just knew I'd find her living here somewhere."

Mrs. Wagoner's eyes never left the swinging locket as she reached out to touch it. Her dark eyes glistened with tears of joy. Taking it from my hand, she held it cupped in her hands close to her heart for a few minutes, then she gently opened it and gazed lovingly at the little face, a miniature copy of herself. "Oh, Rhody, I thank you for this precious gift of love."

"I'll bring the box and the other things to you the next time we're in town." I told her.

I stood watching her and felt tears in my own eyes too, because I realized the face in the locket had become my friend, and now I'd never know her. I was happy for Mrs. Wagoner though, for Mama said that treasured picture will help comfort her and make her feel much better.

Mrs. Wagoner pulled a white hankie from her apron pocket and wiped her eyes, and then with trembling fingers, I watched her carefully remove the small picture. She snapped the locket shut and placed the small picture gently in her pocket, then softly patted her pocket. I wondered why she took it from the locket for it was so well protected in there.

She held out her arms to me and said, "Come here, Rhody." I moved closer. She placed the chain and the locket over my head. The locket hung loosely around my neck; she patted it and said, "There, it's yours. It will be so pretty with your hair." She smiled and kissed my cheek.

In disbelief, my hands reached up to caress the locket, still warm from her touch. I looked up into Mrs. Wagoner's deeply colored eyes, still wet with tears, and whispered softly to her. "Oh, thank you, Mrs. Wagoner, now I can wear it! Now it is really mine!"

I was still in a daze when Mama and I left the store. I turned and waved to Mrs. Wagoner. My mind was in a whirl and when we reached the wagon where Papa and Sidney waited. The first thing out of Sidney's mouth, "You're wearing the locket!"

We told them the entire story. It was like the ending of a fairy tale dream that had come true, but not as I had planned, for now I would never see or know the face that had become my friend and I had come to love.

I wore the locket home and there sat Gabe waiting for us to return. I cried as I told him the unbelievable story of the locket. I confessed to him that I'd never forget that face though, and he licked my tears.

A New Outlook

After knowing I would never meet little Martha or could she ever be my special friend as I had envisioned from the time I found the locket, I was saddened at the thought of her. It seemed though after I realized that she was gone I was not so distracted and my friends at school and church became more real and exciting to me. Soon Sarah Beth became my very best friend, and from the time she and I met, we bonded and remained close friends for all times.

During our early school years at our new home, Sidney and I settled into a routine of school and helping around home, which meant growing up with family values and responsibilities. Those years passed quickly and soon our family became an intricate part of this entire rural community surrounding us.

From the beginning Sidney always enjoyed helping Papa with the farm and the cattle; he seemed to love the land and grew up to become a strong, good-looking, responsible, young man. He was fun to 'buddy' around with when we grew to the age of attending the teenage Friday night parties or socials as we called them, that were planned community activities provided by the parents or the church.

While growing up we only rode Barney to school during bad weather, but as we grew older so did Barney, so more and more we let him enjoy his leisure pasture time and giving Papa a ride once in awhile. We were thrilled and surprised beyond words when Papa gave each of us a good riding horse of our own. When they were brought to us, we saw they were beautiful animals, and it was a total surprise to both of us! The lighter colored one walked directly to me. Papa said, "Rhody, I don't know how she knew, but she was the one I selected for you." My name for her was Sandy for that described her color with a lighter mane.

Sidney's horse was a little darker in color, and he was thrilled almost speechless to have a horse all his own. Guess what he named his horse? Jake! He named him Jake, and we never wondered why.

I kidded him, "Boy, I wonder what Old Jake would think about you naming your horse after him?"

Sidney only grinned, "Aw, I think he'd like it, for he was a real Texas cowboy."

We enjoyed riding with our friends, and having this new freedom entrusted to us. We took good care of our own horse and saddle for they both require a lot of special care. Sidney actually rode his horse more than I, and he often rode with William, our cousin in Norman, so he got to know more of the Norman teenagers than I did. We enjoyed having kids from all around the community join our parties, and we also attended theirs. Verl Anne and Wayne, our cousins often attended the parties and they rode with us on many weekends. Everyone was always invited, so we finally knew most of the kids our age in the area.

These community parties were our primary entertainment for young people at that time. They were fun get-togethers planned by parents to promote social development in their young people.

All these friends and activities quickly filled the vacant place in my heart for the little girl in the locket.

Sidney's Guest

One day, just out of the blue, Sidney asked, "Rhody, are you going to the party Friday night over at the Tucker's?"

"Sure, why do you ask? Mama and Papa are going too. They're helping with the refreshments, and you know they always like Old Fiddler's music. We'll be going early to help."

"Good, I've invited William and he's bringing a friend from Norman, and Rhody, boy are you gonna' be surprised?"

"Why am I going to be surprised? Sidney, have you met Joel Ray?" Did he finally come to the Territory?"

"Oh you just wait and see," he said teasingly.

"Well, I'm glad William is coming for I want him to meet Sarah Beth anyway. I think they will like each other."

We both looked forward to this special Friday night party, and Sidney seemed extra excited about me meeting William's friend. He acted as if he wanted to tell me who it was, but wouldn't, for I could tell he was really excited about it.

We went early to help the Tuckers ready the place for the party; the yard was swept clean, lanterns were placed around hanging on the porch posts, on trees or wherever to lighten up the yard. Light bugs buzzed around the golden light from the lanterns. It looked festive on this warm summer evening.

Papa said, "Rhody, your golden hair glows in this light like corn silk."

"Thanks, Papa. Mama's homemade soap sure gives clean hair a shine."

Soon the young people started arriving. I could hardly wait for Sidney to get here to see who his big surprise might be. I really expected Joel Ray, for I knew most everybody else around here. I was anxious to know who I had not yet met.

When the Old Fiddler got up, placed his fiddle under his chin and started tapping his foot, we knew it was time for the party to begin. We yelled for everybody to come in closer. His group started their music and we gathered quickly to the lively music

144

and singing. Anybody who wanted to sing a solo could sing, sometimes a trio or a quartet would sing, so we had fun listening from the best to the worst. It was all in fun. We played party games out in the yard, then danced, if we wanted to dance awhile, or joined in group singing. Activities were varied and kept moving lively. Lemonade and cookies were always there, for the summer evenings were hot until the cool south breeze blew in about sundown.

About the time we started I finally saw Sidney ride in on Jake with William and his friend following. They tied their horses all together and walked in closer. I motioned to Sarah Beth, "Come on, I want you to meet our cousin, William."

We ran toward them as Sidney motioned wildly for us to come closer, I just knew it would be Joel Ray. I almost stopped in my tracks when I caught sight of the 'face' with him. My heart jumped a beat in my chest. I gasp, "Sarah Beth, he looks like the little girl in the locket . . . exactly like her! That's her face!"

This tall, young man with dark hair and eyes walked toward me, when Sidney said, "Rhody, I want you to meet Dennis Paul Wagoner. This is my sister, Rhody."

He said, "Hi!"

I said, "Hi!" Both of us stood speechless.

Face of Destiny

Right there before me stood William's friend with the exact face of the girl in the locket that I had searched for so long. My hand went directly to the locket suspended around my neck. I squeezed it tightly.

He said, "Rhody, I've wanted to meet you," . . . then hesitated, "you are as pretty as Mom said." He went on, "I want to thank you for returning little Martha's picture to Mom. Getting that picture back really helped her."

I said, "Then you are little Martha's brother? Your mother said they had a son, but I never dreamed you looked exactly like her. I've been in the store several times, but I've never seen you."

"I usually work in the back on Saturday mornings or making deliveries for Dad. Mom told me several times that I'd missed you."

Still holding tightly onto the locket I said, "Your mother gave me this locket, and I wear it all the time. I love wearing it." I repeated, "Your Mom said she had a son, but Dennis, I never dreamed you looked exactly like Martha."

Dennis said, "Yeah, we really favor, I guess, everyone always said we did."

I turned to Sidney, "Why didn't you tell me you knew him?"

Sidney said, "No, no, I didn't know him. I just met Dennis myself. I was as surprised as you when I saw him. I couldn't believe my eyes, so I brought him to meet you. I wanted to tell you the other day, but I also wanted to surprise you." Sidney turned to Dennis, and said, "You don't know how long we looked for your face after we moved here."

We all laughed about it, and William said, "Well, I guess I'm the guilty one. I kind of thought Dennis might be the face you talked about so much, except you always talked about a little girl."

"Yeah, it was a little girl's picture in the locket." I said. "It was his sister's picture."

William confessed, "Well, I had not heard much about it lately, so I guess I had forgotten, but Sidney almost fell out of his saddle when he met Dennis."

Dennis and I kept looking intently at each other. I could hardly believe that I was seeing this real face smiling back at me. As we all stood together getting acquainted, I remembered. "Hey, William and Dennis, I almost forgot to introduce my best friend, Sarah Beth Anders."

William said, "Sarah Beth, I'm glad to know you. Dennis and I know your brother, Brent, real well, but he didn't ever tell us that he had such a pretty sister. Is he here tonight?"

"Yeah, he's around somewhere. Probably with Lee Ann. They're usually together."

I can't tell you what else happened at the party that night. My head was still in a whirl and my heart still spinning with Dennis' face. After I introduced him to Mama and Papa, we all talked, laughed, and danced the rest of the evening.

Papa said, "Dennis, you'll never know how long we searched for your face." We all laughed and enjoyed the story all over again.

All evening my heart reeled every time my eyes looked in Dennis' direction."

He smiled at me. "Oh, that locket looks real pretty on you! Mom will be glad that I've finally met you.

You know, you are a very special girl to her. She's told me over and over that I should meet you and how pretty you are. Now I see that for myself." I kept wondering how we missed meeting each other for so long since we were in and out of the store each Saturday when we were in town? It never occurred to me that their son would look exactly like his sister in the locket, but they were almost identical. They both strongly favored their mother. From the moment my hands touched Dennis' hands that night, I knew I never wanted to let go.

We spent a lot of time together after that first meeting, going to parties on weekends, riding together, enjoying long walks and quiet picnics on weekends. It seemed we were meant to be together, for our attraction appeared to be mutual from the beginning.

I had carried that imprinted face in my heart for so long, and now Dennis stood before me with the face I dreamed of meeting so long—the face I had come to love and didn't know it.

Months passed quickly and we were together as often as we could arrange it, mostly on weekends. We were never disappointed in each other, so over time our lives bonded into true love.

One day we were out riding together and Dennis said, "Come on, let's ride over this way, I want to show you a pretty view where a large tree stands on the hill overlooking the tree-lined river basin land covered with growing crops. It was a fun ride together. We stopped and got off our horses and walked across to the edge where we admired the scene below of rich farming land. As we enjoyed the view of spring and new life, Dennis turned to me and told me again of his love for me, and as we stood close in our own world I sensed something more this time. He took my hands in his and repeated his love for me. He said "I have loved you from the minuteI saw your face." He asked me to marry him that day, pledging his love forever.

I wanted to shout, "Yes" to the top of my voice, for my love for him was so great, but I melted in his arms and pledged my own love to him forever.

I learned he had already talked to Papa and Mama, and had their blessings to ask me to marry him, and would you believe he had also talked to Sidney. How Sidney ever kept that secret from me, I will never understand.

Any time Dennis held me in his arms, or I cupped my hands around his face, I knew that was the face I loved and knew my search was over—my heart sang with happiness.

Epilogue by Sidney

After we moved from Texas, Rhody and I grew up in this close-knit family home that sheltered our lives in this new area. Being two years younger, I was always proud that Rhody was my 'big' sister, for I could see that she was a special girl and one of the prettiest around, small in stature, but with a big, oversized determined spirit.

After meeting Mrs. Wagoner and knowing her little friend in the locket was gone, Rhody still spoke often of her. She was a popular young lady living a care-free, happy life, dating and going to parties with friends, but she never forgot that face. I think it had become an unfulfilled dream that she could not forget.

Rhody still day-dreamed about Joel Ray too, that fifteen year old run-away we helped on the trail. I teased her about him all the time, so that may be why she kept thinking he might actually show up someday. She kept remembering his words, "I'll see you again someday."

I finally grew-up myself and quit teasing her and encouraged her to forget him, for he was three years older than her and I knew that he probably already had a life of his own on a Texas ranch somewhere, but she kept daydreaming about him though, saying, "Oh, he just may show up one day like he said."

After she met Dennis, she said, "Sidney, I don't know why I kept thinking of Joel Ray for so long; I guess I just had this childhood, fanciful dream of him showing up someday as my prince charming on a white horse. I knew in my heart that I would never see him again, but it was a good dream." She laughed and slapped at my hat, "How'd you get so smart all of a sudden?"

There was never anyone else for Rhody after she met Dennis; she never dated anyone else after they met. I don't think either of them ever dated anyone else again. Her heart flipped every time she saw Dennis for he was the face she had loved and longed to meet for so long. The feeling must have been mutual for the two of them, for they dated regularly after that first meeting and were always together at community parties. They fit together like a perfect pair—like a pair of fine gloves.

Dennis worked full time at the store learning his father's trade, and in later years his father made him a full partner in the business, changing the name to Wagoner and Son General Store.

After he and Rhody met, the next year passed quickly for all of us. Dennis proposed and they began planning a summer wedding. Rhody always wanted to be married in Mama's flower garden, and in June when all the lilacs were in full bloom sending their fragrance throughout the air, Rhody got her wish. Papa gave her away to Dennis with all our blessings. She and Dennis married in a beautiful garden wedding with William and Sarah Beth as their attendants in the presence of many friends and family joining the Lawsons and the Wagoners in an event long remembered by the community. It was truly a love story to remember.

Dennis's face had touched Rhody's heart from the moment they met, and in each other they found a never-ending love.

They lived many long, happy years raising their family in the city of Norman, Oklahoma, as Wagoner and Son General Store became a landmark in town generation after generation.

I married my classmate, Sue Ellen, and our two families stayed close for we were bound by strong cords of family love. I leased some good bottom land to farm and raise cattle as my first business venture, and also helped Papa farm as long as he was able. I'd loved that land since I was nine years old and first touched its red soil.

Our two families spent many years of close relationship with each other. Rhody and Dennis were devoted to their own family, and were blessed with long lives together becoming great grandparents. Dennis died first leaving Rhody a widow a few years.

All our children and grandchildren never tired of Rhody's endless stories about moving to Oklahoma in a covered wagon in the year she celebrated her twelfth birthday and I was nine years old. She told them every incident growing up with me and all our lively adventures. The grandchildren's imaginations were always set on edge with the mystery of someone following us on the trail, and our long search for the face in the golden locket that she had found in a little tin box in Indian Territory.

They all huddled around her with gales of giggles and laughter erupting as she delighted them with story after story of when she and I were growing up together. She made the story of the old Indian man and his dog a thriller for them, and they really liked to hear about Gabe, our prairie guardian, who finally showed up to help drag me out of a sink hole. They always wanted to see Old Jake's pocket knife too, for I still carried it, but the mystery of the face in the locket was a favorite story with all of them.

They especially enjoyed the part of her beautiful life story of how one night when she and I were teenagers, I brought someone *special* to meet her at a party. When she first saw him she knew instantly that was the face she had searched for so long. Nothing ever made their eyes shine and twinkle more than when she'd tell them who that *special* face turned out to be at the end.

Rhody always wore her golden locket, and as the story ended each time, she'd click the locket open, and the grandchildren always clapped and roared with laughter when Grandpa's face looked back at them.

Long after everyone had gone home each time, the laughter and happiness lingered on in her heart, as the golden glow from the locket still filled her life, as she remembered again and again the evening she finally met the love of her life—and their real love story began.

CPSIA information can be obtained at www.ICGtesting.com
Printed in the USA
239641LV00001B/8/P